Decoding Us

A Novel about friendship

Erica J Whelton

Publisher: Sunseri Design Publishing
ISBN: 978-1-956069-19-8

Printed in the United States of America

To my wonderful PIMs, especially to our beautiful angel, Heather.
You have saved me more times than I can count.
To the good, the bad, and the ugly.
I'd be lost without you all.

Books by this Author:

Medium with a Heart—Paranormal Cozy Series:
Premedicated Murder (book 1)
Replicated Murder (book 2)
Organized Murder (book 3)
Inherited Murder (book 4)
Crafted Murder (book 5)
Destined Murder (book 6) — Coming Summer 2023

Finding Herself—Women's Fiction Series:
Mandy's Story: Courage (book 1)
Becca's Story: Purpose (book 2)
Caroline's Story: Serenity (book 3)

Paranormal Suspense:
The Haunting of Anna-Rose

A true friend accepts who you are,
But also helps you become who you should be.

Chapter One: Amy

"Screw you, Scott!" I slammed the bedroom door behind me, then stomped my way to the guest room. He wanted to act like that, fine. I could too.

Scott was my third husband. You'd think I could pick them better by now, or at least I'd know what not to do.

But I always fell into the same pattern. In the beginning, we'd be hot and heavy, lust and love. Until about year three or four, then came the screaming, name calling, and cold-shoulders.

We were at the point in our marriage now.

We fought more than we talked, and simple conversations turned into an all out war nine times out of ten. Mostly, it was him making some asshole comment and I would get defensive and bitchy about it.

Tonight's comment was about my weight.

"I get it. I've put on a bit of weight." I snapped with a sarcastic laugh.

"I'm just worried about your health." He tried to backtrack.

"My health? If you were, you wouldn't have said 'watch out, wide load coming through'."

"It was a joke." He laughed, trying to put his arms around me.

"Well, I don't find it funny." I growled and moved away from him.

I remember very little after that because it escalated so quickly. We began bringing up old fights and calling each other names until I grabbed my pillow, my cat, and headed straight to the guest room, slamming the door behind me.

My cat, Archie, slid out of my arms onto the bed, then curled up on the far side. He knew the drill and was unfazed by my tantrum. The poor guy had seen it before.

All the tears, the screaming and the sleepless nights. He usually slept through most of it.

I threw my pillow on the other side and plopped down with a heavy sigh.

"Gawd, I'm so glad my kids aren't here to see me fail again."

I had four kids, though none with Scott. My first three were with Dave and my youngest son, Aiden, was with Carlos.

Recently, Aiden went to live with his father because Carlos lived closer to his school. He was in his sophomore year of college.

Then my other three were grown and moved on, living their best lives. I talked to my three boys once or twice a week. My daughter and I spoke almost daily.

Hannah had recently gotten engaged and would welcome a baby soon. My first grandchild. I had mixed feelings about it.

On the one hand, I was thrilled. A grandchild to spoil and snuggle sounded like so much fun. Those baby years go so fast. I think I blinked, and mine children were grown.

But on the other, I didn't feel old enough to be a grandmother yet. That was for old people.

The truth was, I would turn fifty in just a few months. Plenty old enough to be a grandmother, but I was going to live in denial about my age and future role as grandmother for as long as possible.

My oldest son, Owen, was married. They didn't yet have children, and in his words, they were in no rush.

"We're focusing on our careers right now."

"You'll be working for the rest of your life." I said.

"Yeah, but we'd like to be more financially stable and secure in our jobs."

I tried not to laugh. If everyone waited until they were financially secure, nobody would have children. Or at least I wouldn't. I never could afford mine, but for some reason, I had four of them.

I always figured out how to stretch a dollar. My kids never went without, though at times, I did. It was fine by me; they mattered more. I smiled, thinking back. I'd give almost anything to live, even one of those days again.

My next son, Noah, was not married and didn't look like he cared if he ever did. He was enjoying being single, traveling, and building his career.

He blamed my failed marriages for souring him on relationships. We'd had a few conversations about it.

"Mom, you make it look, well, not fun."

He wasn't wrong and right now, my attitude toward marriage was a negative one. I was sick of fighting and wanted out.

I loved Scott, but the man pushed every one of my buttons and pet all my peeves. But then called me crazy when I reacted to him. He'd say I was too dramatic.

Trying to distract myself from thinking, I grabbed the remote, angrily pushing the power button for the television. Mindlessly, I scrolled through the show options. Settling on a program about a treasure hunt. I didn't even know that was a thing in this day and age.

I cuddled under the blankets, pulling my orange purring friend closer to me. He had been my constant companion for the past ten years. I got him towards the end of my marriage to Carlos. Archie has heard all the ups and downs of my life.

I scratched around his ears and cheeks.

"Sorry to bring you into yet another broken home, buddy. After this, we are done."

He started kneading his paws on my chest, purring as he snuggled up under my chin. Archie was the best cuddler.

With the cat curled up on me, I focused my attention on the show as they talked about this modern-day treasure.

"Several teams have tried, but always get stuck. Unable to find clue three. Tonight, we will talk with a few of those teams to hear about their experience."

Interesting.

Not sure what about it drew me in, but I was hooked.

It was a treasure hunt for ten pirate bust statues. They were created by Michael Carren. He wrote a book about the ten pirates and then commissioned to have these figurines created. He took those and created a treasure hunt, hiding the prizes all around the United States.

There was a website that went along with the book. I did a quick search, only to discover I couldn't see much without registering as a team. What I could find said, that one treasure was buried in Florida.

"I love Florida." I hadn't been in a while and never to the panhandle area. "Close to Pensacola. Nice"

We had mostly spent time near Disney and then in the Tampa Bay area. This would be new and fun. I needed new and fun right now. Between work and home life, I was a mess.

Archie stretched, yawned, then moved away from me.

"Sorry, little buddy."

He was mostly used to my insomnia filled nights, but he had his limits with me. I snuggled into my blankets as I kept reading and searching for information. With the forums locked to members only, I did the best I could to find more details.

What I found had me convinced this was something I could do. Not just could do, wanted to do.

Maybe I should ask a few of my girlfriends to go with me. We could form a team, then I'd be able to access the additional forums.

Like me, they could all use a distraction from life. It was near the beach. We could drink fruity drinks by a pool. I'm sure they would all be on board.

Though they didn't talk about their troubles with me much anymore; I knew they had to have them, right? Everyone did, or at least I assumed they did.

We really didn't share as much with each other as we used to. It seemed to stop once we were done worrying about potty training and skinned knees, or the kids staying out after curfew or where were they going to college.

Back then, we were drawn to the message boards. We found like-minded women among the many topics, birth months, child-rearing methods and styles, and lifestyles. After we got to know each other better, we took it to private forums so we could talk even deeper and privately.

The group was roughly forty women from all walks of life. We met on a message board for the birth year for at least one of our children. For me, it was my youngest.

Through the many years, the group has fluctuated, members came and went. Sometimes they'd come again, but the core group stayed together. They have always been people I could count on no matter what I have going on.

In those early years, we had planned a few big trips to meet in person. They were wildly fun and gave us a chance to bond in a way online didn't. It was magical. You meet these strangers that you know so much about and everything just clicks.

Mostly, all our children were on to the next chapter of their lives, and we were in the less active part of parenting. Because of that, our group was less active online now. We still shared, but over the years, it became more about things like work or where to go on vacation.

Since our kids brought us together, we'd still share about what our kids were doing. We were all invested in the lives of these beautiful humans that felt like nieces and nephews. I had met some of them over the years, which was fun, especially when our kids got to meet each other.

Other than the kids, we shared less and less about ourselves. Though I had shared a little about Scott and me fighting, but it was again surface stuff. Things that weren't a big deal. I didn't share how much I imagined a life without him and just staying single forever.

Maybe I'd get a bunch of cats. I looked over at my sleeping companion. He would hate other cats.

Thinking of my friends again, we were all moms first, women second. A trip would give us a chance to reconnect not only as friends but with ourselves. I knew I couldn't be the only one who needed a break from life.

In fact, we could do this treasure hunt. It would be a fun escape and activity to do as a group. But who could I ask? This didn't feel like a whole group thing.

I thought of my closest friends, Heather, Marissa, and Denise. Heather and I had grown up together. Though neither of us lived in our hometown any longer, we had stayed best friends. We'd met Marissa and Denise online, and almost instantly formed this little group of four from our larger group.

Yes, I'll ask just them to start with. I'll message them tomorrow.

Done with my phone, I put it on the nightstand, then rolled to my side to count sheep until I dozed off. Only to wake less than an hour later and the night of a thousand tosses and turns began. I cursed each time I woke to stare at the clock.

When my alarm went off, I was already sitting up, rubbing the sleep from my eyes and wishing for more hours of sleep. Archie rolled his head to look at me, yawned, and went back to sleep.

I grabbed my phone from the nightstand and then headed to the bathroom. After I relieved myself and washed my face, I headed to the kitchen for coffee.

"Good morning, beautiful." Scott came in, boxers riding low on his hips.

His perfectly sculpted hips, I thought, but damn it all, I was still mad at him, so I forced myself to not look at him. Well, one quick peek. *Damn!*

I mumbled a hello which won me a half-naked man wrapping himself around me.

"Are you still mad? Please, don't stay mad." He kissed my forehead, then kissed his way to my mouth. I was not in the mood, but I gave into his kissing a little.

"You really hurt my feelings." I grumbled.

"You know I didn't mean to."

"I want to believe that, but weight is a sensitive subject."

"Well, come to the gym with me. I can help you get in shape."

He was a gym rat, which was great for him and others, but I didn't want that. He met me when I was overweight; he knew what he was getting into. I hadn't tried to change him; he shouldn't try to change me.

"I'm okay. I just don't need you pointing at my flab."

"Fine." He pulled me closer to him, trying to kiss me. "I love you."

"I love you, too." Lord, help me, I did, but he still pushed my buttons and got me madder than a hornet. Mentally, I stomped my foot. Externally, I offered him a weak smile.

He got his protein shake going while I added creamer to my coffee, which had me feeling guilty. I know I could eat, but I didn't want to. I mentally stomped my foot.

Taking my coffee, I headed to our room to get ready for work. I stared at my clothes for a while, trying to decide how I felt about today. What clothing matched my mood, or maybe what could put me in a better head space for the day ahead? Something not as mundane as my job.

"Blue slacks, cream blouse, red heels?" I muttered to myself as pulled each item out to look at.

"I love you in those shoes." Scott leaned against the door frame.

He wanted sex. I could tell. He always stalked me around the house when he was frisky. I was not in the mood. Whatever the opposite of randy was, *that* is where I was.

"Thanks, babe." I said, as I searched for a casual blazer to wear. It was always cool in the office, so I liked to have some kind of jacket.

Once I was ready, I got my travel mug filled with more coffee and grabbed a granola bar for the road. I ran through my checklist. Keys, purse, laptop, security badge and coffee.

Good to go.

"Bye," I yelled over my shoulder as I headed out the door.

"Wait, babe." Scott chased after me, now in his running shorts and tank top. "Are you really leaving without a kiss?"

I was, but I plastered on a smile.

"Sorry, distracted." I kissed him quickly. "Have a good day."

"You, too."

As I hopped in my car to head to work, I forgave him a bit, but I was still hurt. I had concerns about our marriage, and it was keeping me up at night. This wasn't just a minor issue for me. It wasn't just a kiss and make-up thing.

It, also, wasn't just the comment about my weight. He was always taking jabs at my expense.

When I cleaned, I did it wrong. When I fold the towels, I didn't fold them correctly. My kids were all messed up. His weren't much better. At least none of mine had been arrested, but pointing that out, obviously, caused a fight.

We were older when we met, both stuck in our ways. I don't think we ever adjusted to living with another stubborn person. That is exactly what we are. Two stubborn people stuck in our ways and not giving in to the other.

I groaned, then turned the volume up on the radio, so I didn't have to think. If I thought, I would have to acknowledge that this really was a me issue and not an us or him issue.

When I pulled into work and the dread of having to trudge through another day, the truth slapped me in the face. I was the problem. I simply had a poor attitude about life right now.

Perhaps a vacation was in order, but I definitely needed to add 'find a therapist' to my list of things to do. Also, maybe a hormone check with my doctor, too.

I grabbed my stuff and headed in.

Today was going to be boring. We were right in the middle of budget and resource planning for our project. That meant endless meetings to talking about more meetings and planning how to do the work.

I just wanted to get my team started on the building piece of this, and not distract them with all this planning. My team developed and managed an in-house software. We had a separate process for planning our workload, yet I was still required to sit in these week-long meetings.

It was mind-numbing.

I went to my office to drop off my purse and check my email and schedule for the day.

"Hey, Amy." One of my employees stuck her head in the door.

"Oh, good morning, Nicole."

She was my right hand. My second in charge and kept things going with the team while I wasn't available.

"You still have those planning meetings today?"

"Yes, ugh, kill me now."

She laughed slightly. "What do you need me to do while you're doing that?"

"Can you make sure we have everything for the next release? All the testing needs to be documented, and we need sign off from Bev."

"Got it. Anything else?"

"Um, not at the moment, but my email is just coming up." I darted my eyes to the screen. "What is this from Jerry?"

"Oh, yeah, he wants an urgent change."

"We can't make that change this week."

"I know. I talked to him, but he wants to talk to you."

I sighed dramatically.

"I'll handle it. Thanks. If I get anything else, I'll let you know."

She left me while I caught up on emails, and then looked for where my first meeting was.

Two floors up. I groaned as I gathered my stuff and headed to the first meeting, as my mind daydreamed about white sand beaches and treasure.

Chapter Two: Heather

I sighed as my eyes opened. Another Thursday with nothing to do.

I rolled out of bed, heading straight to the bathroom. Staring at the bags under my eyes, I didn't even recognize myself sometimes. Turning on the cold tap, I splashed the icy water on my face. The coolness felt good on my skin.

I sighed as I made my way to the kitchen to start the coffeepot, then I pulled out my phone, scrolling through old pictures. I missed my boys. They didn't call or text enough. I sent them each a good morning and a wish for a good day before setting my phone down.

My husband, Jason, came in, kissing my cheek. "Are you missing the boys again?"

"Yeah, always." I could try to deny it, but he knew me too well.

"Why don't you try getting out of the house today? See if you can meet a friend for lunch or for shopping, maybe?"

"That's an idea." I smiled.

Though I had no idea who to call. Most of my friends lived in other parts of the country and the few local friends I had worked or had young children still at home. Nobody I could call up for a spontaneous lunch date.

"Well, good. I hope you can."

I studied him for a moment. "Maybe I should try going back to work."

"Yeah, I think that's a great idea. Whatever makes you happy." He smiled, "Alright, I'm off."

He kissed me once more and then he was gone. The already quiet house seemed quieter. The silence was near deafening.

With the boys gone and our dog having passed away a year ago, there was so little for me to do around the house. Jason and I didn't make much mess, at least nothing I couldn't handle in a few minutes each day.

He worked all day, and sometimes traveled for work. This meant I was alone and had almost nothing to do on t.

Like now, he was gone until at least six this evening. That was nearly twelve hours alone in the house. Unless I could find a friend or an errand that needed doing, it would be these same walls that closed in on me day after day.

The worst part is that the longer I was home alone, the more I didn't really want to leave. I had everything I needed here. My friends were in my laptop, and I had a television with all my shows. What else did I need?

I knew what I needed, and I wasn't going to find it by hiding in my house.

With my coffee in hand, I grabbed my laptop and headed into the living room. I could start my job search. But I flipped the TV on to the local news station. It would offer a bit of background noise. I then fired up the computer. When the browser came up, I tapped my mug as I stared at the search box.

"How do I find a job?"

I hadn't worked in over twenty years. *No, wait.* Recalculating in my head, I realized it was actually closer to thirty.

"Twenty-six years, to be exact. Yikes."

I tried one of the job search sites, but when I got to the keyword search, I quickly realized I didn't have any marketable experience or skills. *What do I search for?*

Sure, I could make a mean three-layer chocolate cake with mousse filling that could and has caused a near riot at the church cake walk or organize a room of PTA members into planning the most badass fall festival, but how could I translate that to a paying job?

I typed in Administrative Assistant. That was general enough of a search.

As I read the job postings, they listed things I was good at, but how could I translate my stay-at home duties to work experience?

Things like organizational skills, balancing a budget, and managing the family calendar were skills I had, and people were asking for someone with those skills. But I didn't think doing those things for my family counted as recent experience.

"No. Not that one. Oh, maybe... crap. Five years' experience."

After an hour and two cups of coffee, I gave up. I wasn't suited for anything. They wanted current experience which I didn't have. I couldn't even narrow my search well enough to my skills.

PTA President for eight years looked great in some aspects of life, but in the corporate world, probably not.

Frustrated, I shut the laptop. I looked around at the too large for only two people house.

"Maybe I should get out of the house."

I pulled out my cell phone, looking through my contacts to find someone I could call. Old PTA cohorts, soccer moms, or Sunday school acquaintances. All of them tied to my boys.

My closest friends were my online group of friends that I met on one of those baby care message boards. When I was pregnant with Cody, my youngest, I was scared that I would have another miscarriage. He was my rainbow baby, after miscarrying between him and his older brother, Tyler.

My best friend, Amy, who I'd known since kindergarten, is the one who told me about this site. The many boards divided by topics had been a lifesaver. I was dealing with a preschooler and a high-risk pregnancy. It was nice to log on any time, day or night, and someone was there to offer a few words of encouragement or a virtual hug.

That's where I met my tribe. Then we met Marissa and Denise. We had bonded during our pregnancies. Though none of them had lost a baby, they were so supportive as I made my way through the milestones, breathing a sigh of relief when I finally saw his sweet little face.

We had gotten to meet in person several times over the years, and I talked to them almost daily for years. Though in the last few years, we didn't talk nearly as much.

I sent them a happy Thursday text message then went to shower, so I had no excuse not to leave the house, even if I meant just wandering the aisles of the craft store.

After I was showered and dressed, I checked my phone to find all three had replied with loving messages.

Amy: Happy Thursday! :)

Marissa: Luv u

Denise: Have a good one

That put a smile on my face. I grabbed my purse and headed to the store. Maybe I'd find a new hobby, or at least a jigsaw puzzle. We used to leave one out on the formal dining table, doing a few pieces or more any time we'd walk by. Cody was my master puzzle guy. When he was little, he could whip through a puzzle in just minutes.

I chuckled at the memory. He used to be so proud of himself. Now he was a mechanical engineering student and had his internship lined up for the summer, which meant this was the first summer he wouldn't be home at all.

Tyler was equally smart, but in different ways. He could remember facts and figures from years ago. I loved and hated playing trivia games with him because he knew a lot of random facts.

He was graduating this year from his under-graduate work and would go on to law school. It was the perfect job for him.

I parked at the craft store and headed in. At the door, I grabbed a cart, even though I doubted I would buy enough to justify one. It just gave me a social buffer and something to do with my hands.

I started in the seasonal items. Valentine's Day was a few weeks ago, and they had a few shelves with heavily discounted items on it. Maybe I could pick a few things to make a wreath for next year.

But, unfortunately, after browsing through the section, I found it was heavily picked over, so I moved on.

Next, I browsed the Easter items. At home, I had a box full of Easter decor, but it was fun to look at everything. I thought back to when the boys were little. I used to make large baskets filled with trinkets and treats.

A young mother with a toddler riding in the cart was looking at Easter stuff, too. I listened to the child babble about the bunnies and chicks.

"Egg?" She pointed to a large plastic egg.

"Yes, that's an Easter egg."

"Bunny? Brown bunny."

"Yes, that's a brown bunny."

I smiled as I walked past them. *Oh, how I missed my boys.* Nobody tells you how fast that time really goes. I mean, they say it goes fast, but not at light speed. Here I am, not feeling like a mother any longer, even though I've been one for nearly twenty-six years.

Leaving that section, I continued on through the store, but nothing jumped out at me. I'd already tried knitting and crochet. Making jewelry came after that. It didn't stick. Nothing did.

But I was determined to find something to do. Turning to the aisle with all the prepackaged craft kits. I browsed until something caught my attention.

"Watercolors? Now this looks fun."

I picked up it to see what was included. A few brushes, some paints, and a pad of watercolor paper. Interesting. I tossed it in the cart, then kept browsing to see if anything else sparked the creative bug.

I got to the home decor section. My favorite. I loved the knick-knacks and funky artwork.

"Oh, this would look great in Tyler's apartment." I peeked at the price of the splashy red and orange painting. "Sixty-five. Yikes."

But it would be a great birthday gift so I put it in the cart. I didn't bother to look for Cody. He wasn't in a settled place yet. Not like Tyler.

Checking the time, I was shocked to see that only an hour had passed. It still had about nine to ten hours to go.

But with nothing left to look at, I headed to the checkout with my watercolor kit and the picture for Tyler.

"Find everything, okay?" The cashier asked.

"Oh, yes, thank you."

"Watercolors. Fun."

"Yeah, trying something new." I smiled.

"We offer a class once a month."

"Oh, really. I'll have to look into that."

That could be fun, though it was only once a month. Perhaps I could research other classes, even something at the community college. Continuing education was a thing. It was an idea.

Back in my car, I sat staring for a minute.

What now?

I scanned the parking lot, trying to decide my next move. It was April, but perhaps I could walk around the outlet mall to do some early Christmas shopping. I'd gotten a birthday gift for Tyler, but Cody's was next month, long before Ty's.

Alright, that's what I'm going to do. Retail therapy, then take myself to lunch. It wasn't something I was comfortable with, but it beat being at home alone, waiting for my purpose to knock on the door.

I put the car in gear and headed towards the mall. An 80s song came on the radio.

"Oh, yeah, this is my song here." I laughed, cranking the volume.

I sang along, which gave me courage when I finally pulled into the outlet mall's parking lot minutes later. Stepping out, I could feel the weather was ready to change. The news station had mentioned it might rain.

I shrugged and made my way from the parking lot to the open area mall, walking past several stores before deciding to step into the candle store. The floral, fruity, spicy smell hit me. I took a deep breath. I loved this smell.

"Welcome!" a lady called out from the floor as she unloaded a box of candles onto the bottom shelf.

"Thank you."

I browsed around, smelling this one or looking at the bright colors in another. Everything smelled so good. I wanted to buy half the store, but decided on a citrus one. The fruity scent reminded me of a fresh orange. On my way to the register, a tea light set caught my eye.

This is cute. I could give it as a gift. Maybe to my sister-in-law.

I paid and then headed to the kitchen supply store, even though I didn't need a thing, but it was packed with things fun things to browse through. I always found something cute or quirky.

As I was examining a set of fruit shaped measuring cups, I heard someone call my name. I turned to see Valerie Ackland. Internally, I screamed.

Her daughter, Kayla and Cody used to date. Cody said it was casual, but Kayla was head over heels for him. It did not end well.

"Oh, hi, Valerie."

"It's so nice to see you." She leaned to hug me.

"Yes, nice to see you. It's been a while."

"It has." She smiled. *"How's Cody?"*

Her tone was not lost on me. When the two teens broke up, he immediately started dating someone new. Kayla was crushed. Valerie had called me, all upset and bitching me out. I had tried to talk to him about being sensitive to her feelings, but he hadn't listened.

"He's doing well. Enjoying school and has an internship lined up for this summer." I paused. I tried to keep my tone humble. "How is Kayla?"

"She is doing marvelously. She is finishing her nursing program and was recently offered a position over at Central Hospital. She's dating a wonderful young man, and she's happy."

Her tone held a challenging tone, as if she was baiting me to say anything about Cody's love life. Honestly, even if I thought to share it with her, he didn't tell me about his dates anymore. Not after all the drama and mom lectures he'd gotten.

"That's wonderful. I'm happy for her and congratulations on her nursing job."

She smirked. "So, what are you up?"

"Oh, just a little shopping. Nothing special. You?"

"I'm meeting some girlfriends shortly. Just wasting sometime until lunch."

"That's nice."

"Yes." She looked me up and down. "I better get over there before this rain starts. Take care, and it was *so good to see* you."

"You too." *Not.*

I watched her go. She waved just before she moved completely out of sight. How arrogant of her to think I was still looking, even if I was. *Rude.*

I set the measuring cups back on the shelf and continued exploring the store, but my mind was distracted. If she was meeting friends for lunch, clearly, there were other stay-at-home moms or women that got together. So why didn't I have any? What was wrong with me?

Jason had told me I'd gotten my identity so lost in raising our boys that I had forgotten how to make friends or that I even needed to do that. If not for my online group of friends, I would have no one, well, except for Jason, but he worked a lot.

I shook off the encounter with Valerie and tried not to think about how I was suddenly feeling like a loser with no friends. Reminding myself I had Amy, Marissa, and Denise, at least. They didn't live close enough to grab lunch or get our nails done together, but I could count on them when I needed a friend to talk to.

From the kitchen store, I went to the shoe store, looking at all the cute shoes I didn't need was fun. I tried on a red pair of strappy heels. I practically moan at the look of them. Sexy and sparkly, but I had no use for them. I tried on a cute pair of brown sandals that would go with a new sundress I had bought for Easter.

I squealed quietly as I got them. Heading to the register, I had a little bounce in my step. New shoes could do that to a person.

Once I had paid, I stepped out of the store just as the sky opened up.

"Great." I mumbled.

I hadn't thought about bringing my umbrella. I looked left and then right. No restaurants convenient and since I didn't know where Valerie was going for her lunch, I decided just to go home. I took a deep breath and made a run from awning to awning as I tried to make my way back to my car.

I stood under the last bit of cover before I hit the parking lot. Giving a short laugh, I sprinted the last few yards to my car. I got in soaked but laughing.

It had turned out not to be such an awful day. I just had to get through the next five hours alone. I could do it.

Chapter Three: Marissa

Today I had a full schedule of meetings and a client lunch, then the girls had voice lessons tonight. Plus, I had a ton of errands to handle in between. The morning flew by and so did lunch with the potential new client.

As the CEO, I normally didn't go to lunch with our clients any longer. I had a sales team for that, but this one had been a hard fish to catch. We had done everything in our playbook to win their business.

Unfortunately, to date, it hadn't worked, and we really wanted this client. If they signed to use our HR software, it would be our largest client and make up 20 percent of our profit for the year. That's where I step in.

"So, whaddya think?" I said after the bill was settled and we were ready to head out.

"It all sounds excellent." John, the CEO said. "You've made us feel really comfortable that this is the right decision for us."

"You're going to sign up, then?"

"Yes, I think we will."

"Wonderful. I'll have my sales department get with your team." I put out my hand to shake his. He did the same.

Deal done. We said our goodbyes. I shot off a text to Elliot, my assistant, so he could start the ball rolling.

I've got to make a few stops before I get back.

K

My first stop was the dry cleaners to pick up mine and my husband's items. It was a weekly chore that I hated. When I parked, I noticed a new sign stating they offered delivery.

Yes! I grabbed the current drop-offs and went in.

"Good afternoon, Ms. Marissa." The owner, Jackie, greeted me.

"Good afternoon. Here to pick up." She took my slip.

"Alright, let me get these for you."

She called the hanging conveyor system to life, the various items inching forward as she looked for my items.

"Here you are." She hung them in front of me.

"Thanks, Ms. Jackie." I checked a few things. "I'm so glad you got that stain out of his pants."

"You're welcome. I'll have this batch ready tomorrow."

"Saw the sign. So, can I set up a delivery?"

"Of course, of course. I had to give that son of mine something to do with his time besides live on my couch." She laughed.

"I hear that." I laughed.

She then began typing my information into the computer, and we set up my credit card on file. "That's it. We will pick up new items and drop off clean."

"Thanks so much." One less thing on my already too full to do list.

From there, I swung through the pharmacy to pick up my parents' meds. They both had gotten a new one added, for different aliments, so they weren't yet set up to be delivered like most. With my errands run, I pulled through the drive-thru of Beans for an iced coffee. I still had a long afternoon of work, followed up by an endless night of chores. The extra shot of caffeine and sugar would help.

Work was fairly easy for me these days. I had a good team around me and an amazing assistant who seemed to sense when I needed him to step in. He was worth every penny I paid him.

At home, it was my husband and I, plus three of our four kids, and had recently taken in my parents. They couldn't live on their own any longer and we had an enormous house.

Until my parents, Lenny and Sandra, moved in, we were considering downsizing. However, now, we needed every bedroom and bathroom we could get.

My oldest, Emma, was the only one of my children not living at home. She had another year of college and lived in an apartment with two roommates. She worked part-time and was probably my least needy. Though, sadly, I rarely saw or talked to her.

My son, Jackson, hadn't moved out as we'd expected. He was in college, but was doing it all online, so I'd be lucky to even see him most days. Though when it came to food and money, he managed to find me.

Then my youngest daughters, Olivia and Ella, were both still in high school. Olivia was a Junior and Ella a freshman. With their activities, like dance, volleyball for Olivia, and theater for Ella, I was always on the move.

My cell phone rang just before I got back to the office. Answering with the car's bluetooth.

"Hello?"

"Mom!" Olivia's panicked voice filled the car.

"Olivia, what's wrong?"

"You didn't forget, did you?"

Of course I had because I had no idea what she was talking about.

"Forget? Forget what?"

"You were supposed to give me money for the dance team's trip." She whined. It was like nails on a chalkboard.

"Olivia, I left the check at home."

"I didn't get it. Where?"

"Right with your backpack. On top of it."

"There was a paper. I threw it away."

"That was the check, the money for your trip."

I wanted to bang my head on the steering wheel. Where did I fail her that she didn't know what a check was? I needed a checklist of everything I was supposed to teach them and have them initial once we've covered each topic. It would be good when these situations came up. I could point to the list and say, 'told you so.'

"Well, I didn't know. It looked like trash, so I threw it away."

"You need to pay better attention, but I can't bring you a check right now. I'm just pulling into work."

"Why didn't you bring it while you were out doing *whatever*? I need that money, or Ms. Schultz says I can't go."

"Because I gave you a check this morning."

"No, you gave me paper. I don't even know anyone that uses that. Everyone else got it via a cash app to them. Why can't you do that?"

"Because that's not how things work."

"You mean in your old-fashioned mind. Mom, this trip is important! I have to go. I'm a team leader."

"Fine, Liv, I'll be right there." I turned my car out of the parking lot. I would just call my assistant to rearrange my afternoon.

"You're the best!"

I chastised myself for the entire fifteen minutes to her school. She would never learn if I just kept bailing her out, but I also knew how important this was. Not only to her, but to her team and for her college applications.

I knew I would never let her fail, or Ella, for that matter. Though somehow my youngest of four children was my most responsible of them all. It was like she was a middle-aged woman in a teenager's body, at least most of the time. She had her moments of teenaged angst.

She had been the easiest baby, the best-behaved child, and the dream teen. She never missed an assignment in school, never needed me to drive fifteen minutes out of my way to bring her something that I had already brought her. My biggest issue was how she wanted to try everything. If there was a new activity or hobby to try, Ella was all in for it.

She was currently in dance, voice, theater, band, and played soccer. Luckily, right now soccer was in off-season, but she still worked out and practiced with her teammates a few times a week. But she was a good kid, so I ran her around.

The other three could barely keep their heads attached to their bodies without me. Same with my husband and parents. I felt like the glue that was keeping everyone and everything together. And, if I was the family's glue, Ella was mine.

I pulled up at Olivia's school, shot off a text to her, before running inside.

"Hello, Mrs. Martinez." The school secretary greeted. "For Olivia?"

"Hi, yes." I pulled out my checkbook and quickly scribbled it out. "Here you go. I sent her a text that I was here."

"Great. She's been up here five times looking."

"I'm sorry. I gave her a check this morning. She didn't take it."

"No problem. All the kids are like that. I promise." She chuckled. "I'll make sure she gets it."

"Thank you, Mrs. Grady."

I shot off another text to Olivia, then headed back to work. I had already missed my 1 o'clock meeting, but I could still make the one at two. It was the more urgent of my meetings. This one was with my newest accounts manager. He would oversee all new business contracts, like the one I had secured over lunch.

I owned a technology company. We created and maintained a Human Resources software that allowed for all things HR related. From hiring to retirement, and everything in between.

I parked my car, and then jogged to the front doors. Greeting my security staff as I badged through, getting to my office with 30 seconds to spare.

It wasn't until Charles, the new manager, sat down that I realized I should have been a minute late. But for now, the restroom would have to wait until after my meeting.

Two hours later, Charles left the office, and I sprinted to my private bathroom. An awesome perk of being the boss. It offered me a bit of privacy, so nobody heard my slight sigh of relief. With having four kids, I didn't need to give my bladder such a scare. It was already iffy when I laughed or coughed.

With that need behind me, I checked my emails. I answered those that my assistant couldn't, e-signed a few documents, and reviewed the company-wide communication that would go out at the end of the week. While I did that, my cell phone chimed.

It was dad.

Dad: Mom wants to know when you'll be home
Me: By 5.

Dad: She'll be ready.

I wanted to tell him to check the board, but it was too confusing for them. Even after more than a year at our house, they still didn't understand my calendar system. Truth be told, nobody in my house seemed to understand it, except Ella. My sweet, more mature than her age, Ella.

I smiled at the picture of my four from years ago. They were nine, seven, four, and two in the picture. They were eating popsicles on our patio, and I caught them sharing a laugh. The kind only siblings understood, and maybe the mom standing close by.

"I miss those days."

"Do you need me?" Elliot stuck his head in the door.

"Oh, no, sorry." I checked the time. "Actually, I need to get going. The girls have various... things."

"Great. Well, I'll see ya tomorrow." He gave a salute and then went back to his desk.

I packed up my stuff and sprinted out of the building. I would have to work a bit later tonight, but for now, my workday was over.

I headed to the school to pick up the girls. Olivia from dance practice, Ella from band.

"Did you get the check?" I asked the second Liv was in the car.

"Hi, mom, how are you?" Olivia mocked.

"Hi, Olivia, how are you and did you get the oh-so-urgent-that-I-had-to-turn-my-life-upside-down-to-bring-you check?"

"First, yes, and second, you wonder where I get my attitude from?"

"Hi, mom," Ella said with a smirk on her face.

"Hi, Ella-May." I drove from the curb. "We have to go get grandma."

"Ugh, does she have to come? Don't you get enough of her at home?" Olivia grumbled.

"Olivia Jane, that is your grandmother and my mother. She is old and gets confused, but she loves to get out of the house, so yes, yes, she does have to come."

"I like when grandma comes. She won't be around for always, and she loves us," Ella said, as she looked out the window. Wise beyond her years.

"Kiss ass," Olivia mumbled.

"Language!" I snapped.

"Whatever, it's not like you don't curse."

"I'm a middle-aged mom of four, CEO of a company that I built, and caring for your grandparents now. I have earned those bad words. You, my dear, have not." I tried to tease her, but she just stewed from the passenger seat. I let it go. I didn't have the energy for her sass today.

We pulled into our driveway.

"Pit stop. This bus is pulling out in five minutes."

The girls hopped out and ran into the house. I made my way in. Kissing my mom and dad on their foreheads.

"I'm going to run to the bathroom, mom. Do you need to go before we leave?"

"Where are we going?"

She was getting more and more confused each day. I needed to consider bringing in help during the day to give my dad a break. I'd add it to my growing list of things that needed to get done.

"We're taking Olivia and Ella to their voice lessons, and then we need to stop for dance shoes for them."

"Oh, okay." She tried to stand.

"No, stay there. I'll be right back to help you up." I smiled weakly at dad.

I ran to my room. I wanted out of these heels and work clothes. I threw on some jeans, tennis shoes, and an oversized sweatshirt. Then ran into the bathroom to once again give my bladder a break. After my hands were washed, I put my hair up into a messy bun.

Heading into the kitchen, I grabbed some water bottles and a couple of granola bars.

"Ready, mom?" I asked, coming back into the living room.

"Yes, where are we going?"

"We're going on a car ride." I smiled.

No point telling her again. She wouldn't remember. I helped her stand. As we walked to the front door, I grabbed her a sweater.

"Bye, dad. Mike should be here soon."

"No problem. I'll probably take a quick nap." His eyes appeared heavy as he spoke. I sure hope he was feeling okay.

I got mom all buckled into the car, then added the bottles of water to the cup holders.

"I brought you a bottle of water. I'm going to put it here."

"Why are you talking to me like I'm a child? You know I raised you."

There's my mom. I knew she was in there, but sometimes doesn't show her face. Her sassy attitude is where Olivia and I got ours from. I missed that version of my mom so much.

"Yes, mom, I remember." I chuckled.

Now we waited. Bless her soul, Ella was the first of the girls out of the house.

"Olivia is in the bathroom doing her hair and make-up." Ella reported. "Hi, grandma."

"Hi, Emma."

"No, I'm Ella." She smiled.

"Oh, right, of course. You look so much like your older sister."

Ella settled in. I honked the horn. That earned me a dirty look from a moody Olivia, who was just coming out of the house.

"Gosh, mom, I was right there."

"Yeah, sorry, I don't have x-ray vision."

We drove quietly to the girls' lesson. They hopped out. Now it was just mom and me to sit and wait.

"Where are they going again? I keep forgetting." Mom rubbed her head. "It gets so confusing."

"I know. They're going to their voice lessons."

"Voice lessons?"

"Yes, for singing. They both enjoy theater and singing."

"They do have lovely voices."

We talked a little, but mom grew quiet. She did this sometimes. So, while she stared out the window, I pulled out my phone and read new emails, answering a few, and then I reviewed the presentation that Elliot had put together for me.

That took me to the end of the girls' lesson, then we made a quick trip to the dance studio for shoes.

Then we headed home. Mike had ordered in Chinese, so we sat to eat. Not much conversation over dinner, unless Jackson made a rare appearance.

"Hey, Jack." I said, when he came in.

"Sup." He nodded. He grabbed a plate full of food and turned to leave.

"No, no, nope. You can't live in your room twenty-four, seven. Sit."

"*Mooommm*. I have worked all day and I have a few hours of homework."

"You heard your mother. Sit." Mike winked at me when Jackson plopped in a chair.

He inhaled his food and any attempt to engage him in conversation was met with a stare. I finally held my hands up to signal I was done trying. He finished and left.

I would be glad when he was done with school and out of the house. He was doing well in school and working full time, so I shouldn't complain about him. I guess I just missed the little boy Jackson, who loved to cuddle and play games with me.

Ella helped clean up dinner while Olivia ran to her room. Mike and Dad went to the den to play video games. Mike had gotten dad hooked on some zombie hunting game, and that is all dad wanted to do when he didn't have to care for mom.

I got mom her after dinner pills and dismissed Ella.

"I can finish cleaning. I'm sure you have homework."

"Yes, tons. Thanks, mom, you're the best."

Then it was just me and mom left in the kitchen. She smiled and watched me clean up.

"You look tired, daughter." Mom said just as I finished cleaning.

"I'm okay."

"I know I'm a handful, but we appreciate all you do for us."

When mom was here, I loved it. Back in her day, she was a spunky, sassy businesswoman. She was the reason I was running my own company now. She had set a wonderful example of having it all. Studying her now, I wondered if this is why she was sick now.

"Wanna go watch them kill zombies?"

"Not even a little bit, but sure, let's go."

"Me neither, but it makes your dad happy."

"It does."

We laughed. It was a beautiful sound to hear her relaxed.

I helped her up, and we joined our men in the other room. While Mike and Dad killed zombies, mom dozed on the couch, so I got out my laptop and got prepared for the next day's work.

It never ended.

Chapter Four: Denise

Today was a day I had been dreading ever since my doctor called to give me the news that I had an abnormal colonoscopy, so now I was sitting in the waiting area for a CT scan.

"We aren't telling you that there is anything to worry about." My doctor had said. "We just want a different view on it."

Of course, I knew they had taken a few polyps during my procedure. They had sent them off for a biopsy. That was two days ago. I didn't know how long those took to come back. I planned to ask today as soon as got the chance.

Fear didn't even begin to describe how I felt right now.

What if this was cancer? What would I do?

I was a single mom with a daughter, Sidney. She was recently married and in her final year of college. Though she was plenty old enough to not need me for daily care, like she once did, my concern was I didn't want her to worry about me. She was starting her own life, and didn't need to be thinking about me.

In fact, I didn't want anyone to worry about me, which was the exact opposite of how my mother had been in life. She wanted everyone to stop whatever they were doing to wait on her hand and foot. Having to be the center of attention in every situation. When I was pregnant with Sid, you would have thought my mother had something to do with it, too. I didn't argue, though; it wasn't worth it.

But it had made me work extra hard not to be a burden on others, or maybe it was just that she had conditioned me to only think of other's needs over my own. Whatever the reason, I never wanted to pressure my daughter or friends with my problems. This was my issue to deal with.

So here I sit, waiting to be called back for the scan and then wait for an undetermined amount of time for the results.

"Ms. Bennett?"

"Here." I raised my hand, for some reason. I would have laughed at myself if I wasn't so damn nervous.

I gathered my purse and walked on wobbly legs to the changing room. The nurse instructed me to undress completely and put on the gown.

"Then you can lock your things in a locker. There are instructions on the wall on how to set a passcode for the locker. Then have a seat in the next room and you'll be called back soon."

"Thank you." I muttered.

The lump in my throat was preventing me from saying more. I was going to cry before the end of today, no matter what the outcome of all of this was. I just didn't know yet if it was going to be tears of joy or sorrow.

I undressed, avoiding the mirror. I knew if I saw the panic in my eyes, I might just run and not look back.

As I opened the gown, I fumbled with figuring out which way to put it on. These things are so confusing, especially when your mind is going a million miles a minute playing the what if game. Finally, I got the gown on, folded up my clothes and then walked to the locker area.

"Crap. A code?"

The nurse had told me that, but I was barely listening before. I guess the last four of Sidney's social security number. Following the directions, I punched in the code, loaded my clothing and purse into it. Once it was shut and locked, I typed the code, and it opened back up.

Okay, good. I thought as I shut it again.

I went to the next room to wait. There was one other lady there. She looked from the television to me, flashed a weak smile, then turned back to the TV. It was clear by her glassy eyes; she wasn't watching it, but was likely playing the what if game as well.

I sat with my back to the wall, facing the door that a nurse or tech would come through to get me when it was my turn.

How had I gotten here?

I tried to eat right, but if I were honest with myself, I ate shitty. Fast food or takeout most nights, especially when Sid was growing up, convenient was the way to go. She had been a picky kid, and I didn't have money or time to waste on foods she wouldn't eat. Full belly became my motto. It sucked, I know, but I was mostly in survival mode back in those days.

Just get through today. Worry about tomorrow, tomorrow.

Now, it was tomorrow and being overweight and unhealthy came to collect. It appeared the collection fee was cancer. I know that wasn't the only way to get cancer. There were so many factors, but I couldn't help but think of something I could have controlled or something I'd done wrong.

After the doctor had called, I had looked up my symptoms that had initially brought me into the doctor. She'd suggested that I have the colonoscopy, given that I was now forty-nine and having symptoms.

"We are recommending at age 45 now, so you are a little over that, but still good, of course."

Who knew gas and constipation could lead to this?

The other lady was called back. I'm not sure how long it would take for her testing or if we were even here for the same type.

Before putting my cell phone away, I had gotten a greeting text from my friend, Heather. It had been a group text between my core group of friends, which also included Amy and Marissa. I thought about it now. It made me smile.

She was one of many friends that I'd met on an online forum years ago. There was a group of us who met on the same message board when we were pregnant or had a newborn. Our babies were now grown.

Over the years, we had gotten together for trips as a larger group and in smaller groups. The four of us hadn't gotten together, just us in a few years. With life and work, it hadn't been a priority, and now thinking about the uncertainty of my future, what if I didn't get another chance to see them?

I looked at the door, willing it to open or burst into flames. If it caught fire, I could put this off a while longer. It neither opened nor caught fire, so I was stuck here waiting.

But no matter how this goes down, I would make more time for my friends. That was my promise. But if this went the way I thought it was going, I might avoid them, at least for a while. Again, my upbringing and belief that I didn't want to be a burden.

"Ms. Bennett?"

"Yes." I stood.

I pushed forward even though it felt like I was walking through wet cement. It was going to be okay. I had to keep repeating that to myself. But my legs wanted to run anywhere but here.

I would fight for Sidney. She needed a mom. I needed her. I didn't even have grandchildren yet.

I could feel the tears waiting to burst forward, but I held them for now as I followed the tech through a mini maze past offices and exam rooms. I thought about all the other patients, many going through similar journeys as I was now. I said a brief prayer for all of them.

"Here we are. Lay with your head towards the machine. Arms by your side and your legs on the wedge."

I climbed up on the table, wiggled until I was in the correct position. The technician adjusted me slightly. Then gave a few instructions that I could barely hear over my beating heart. On autopilot, I agreed to whatever the technician said.

He disappeared from my sight, then I heard the machine start and I began moving into it. While the scan was happening, I pretended I was somewhere else, anywhere else. White sandy beach or a cold mountain cabin, it didn't matter. Just not waiting to hear if I had cancer.

I don't know how long the scan took, but soon it was over and the tech was walking me back to the dressing area.

"Okay, get changed and then go through the door labeled 'to office.' Have a seat in that waiting room and the doctor will be with you shortly."

"Thank you."

Punching in the code I'd created earlier; I gathered my things and went to one of the dressing stalls. As I dressed, I allowed myself to look at my reflection. The green eyes staring back at me looked hollow, scared, wild. I had seen that look on many a face as I worked with troubled youth and battered women.

I will not cry here. Not yet anyway.

I smoothed my blouse, checked my hair, and tried not to think about what awaited me in that next room. This was the least fun maze ever.

I threw the gown into the laundry hamper and then went out the door labeled 'to office' and was met with yet another waiting room. This one had six people in it. Not all looked scared. Some had smiles.

I sat in a corner seat furthest from the door, which I assumed would soon have a person calling my name. As I saw others using their cell phones, I pulled mine out.

A message from Sid. She had an important test today and had gotten a near perfect score. I replied with a congratulations gif.

Then there were a ton of messages between my friends. It was started by Amy asking if we had time to meet tonight. Heather had replied she could, but Marissa was a no.

Amy: How about tomorrow?

Marissa: Tomorrow night works.

Heather: Me too. Pretty much anytime.

I added I was free tomorrow night as well.

Amy: Great! I'll send you all an invite.

Next, I checked my work emails. I answered a few, responded to a meeting request for today with a decline. I let the organizer know I would be back in the office tomorrow.

"Ms. Bennett?"

I stood and followed the nurse to the next level of hell.

"Dr. Ruiz will be with you in a moment." She said after getting me settled in the exam room.

"Thank you."

After she had left me, I looked around the room. Posters lined the wall about different cancers and treatments for them. That got my heart pounded again. I knew this was going to be what they said. I just knew it. Tears formed in my eyes, so I stood to grab a tissue from the box.

Just then there was the knock at the door, and it opening.

"Ms. Bennett." She looked at me standing in the middle of the room in mid-pull. "We can move those closer to you."

"Am I going to need them?"

She hesitated, so I grabbed the entire box. The rest of the appointment was a blur as she explained the tumor they had found and the treatment options. Also explaining, they saw some shadow hinting that it may have spread, so they would like to start treatment.

"Sooner rather than later is recommended. We think we have caught it early enough that you have a good prognosis."

My voice caught in my throat as I tried to speak, but I could barely get out two words.

"How... when?"

"I'll give you some time to think about it, but in the next month or two, we should get you scheduled for treatments. It can take some time to get on the schedule, but this is a fairly slow spreading cancer, so a few days to a week to process will be fine."

"Okay."

"Do you have a support system? Family, friends?"

"Yes."

I choked out, but the truth was, I would only burden them if absolutely necessary. Meaning if I had to have someone drive me or something, even then, I would avoid telling them as much as possible. But my closest friends didn't even live close enough for those things. I think Heather was the closest to me and that was roughly two hours away. It would be too much for a burden to ask for a ride to the doctor.

"Good. During this, those with a good support system have done so much better than those without."

"Okay." Crap. My support system was wonderful. I guess I'd need to think about including them in this. There were things I needed to live for.

"Do you have questions?"

I had a million, but right now, I was struggling to say more than a word or two.

"No, not at this time."

"Okay. I know this is a scary time, but we have staff available to provide counseling and I will be here for you every step of the way." She squeezed my hands. "Follow me out and I'll give you the aftercare summary and some information on the next steps."

Numbly, I followed her out of the room. She handed me a stack of papers.

"Again, don't hesitate to reach out to us and then call this number to get scheduled." She pointed to the highlighted number on one page. "Soon, okay?"

"Okay."

I walked to my car, put my car in gear, and drove away. Not a tear fell until I walked through my front door. I slid down the back of the door into a puddle of despair on the floor.

My life was over. It was done.

I hadn't heard all the hope or treatments. At that moment, I had given up. I laid there crying for over an hour, before I pulled myself up and went to make a cup of tea and wash my face.

In the kitchen, I started my electric water kettle and then grabbed a clean towel from the drawer. I wet the towel and patted my face with it. The icy water felt so good. I dried it and then turned to get a mug and a tea bag.

With the tea brewing, I took my mug into the living room and turned on some trashy TV shows. An hour later, I felt a bit better. I went to look in the fridge for some dinner, settling on a bowl of cereal and some apple slices.

This was one of my favorite things about being single. I didn't have to worry about another person for my meals. I just ate what and when I wanted.

On the flip side, I didn't have anyone here to talk to about my fears or distract me from my worst-case thinking. A shoulder to cry on. Though I wouldn't want them turning their life upside down for me, the bit of comfort would be nice.

I sighed, clearing my bowl and then taking myself to bed. Tomorrow was another day to worry about my future.

Chapter Five: Amy

I was so excited. Tonight, I would propose the treasure hunting trip to my friends. Yes, I could have sent them all an email or group message, but I wanted to see their faces when I suggested it.

We hadn't had a trip together in a few years. The last one had been over a weekend, but what I was proposing was a week by the beach and the treasure hunt would just be a fun activity.

I had already started researching rental houses in the area. I had it narrowed down to three, but leaning heavily towards a four bedroom with beachy theme, a pool, and an unobstructed view of the gulf, which was less than a five-minute walk across a street. It wasn't a public street, so it should be quiet.

Since Heather had been the only one available, I had a whole other day to prepare what I would say and give them some of the logistics. Not to mention, I wanted to take this trip soon, very soon.

I needed a mental health break, because between work and home, I was maxed out. Even though both major things in my life were causing stress, I knew deep down it was mostly a me problem.

Five years ago, I had lost my best friend in the entire world, my grandmother. She had been my rock. My mother and father both worked, so my grandmother kept me during the days and many weekends I would stay the entire weekend. It was the best. I helped her with cooking and working in her garden. I was her little princess.

When I started school, she was the one to drop me off and pick me up each day, then stayed with me until one or both of my parents came home. Then when my folks divorced, I was devastated. My grandmother offered for me to stay with her until the dust settled and I felt ready to deal with them.

As a teenager, I rebelled, which I know hurt her, but she stayed steady and strong, supporting me no matter what. Now, having gone through the teen years with four children myself, I know what I put her through was hurtful. I had tried to apologize once, but she wouldn't let me.

"Sweetie, I was a teen once. Nobody could have told me anything. Teens are just that way. I love you and that's the past."

Oh, how I missed her. She had helped through all the sleepless nights with my children and even helped me by babysitting them. It had given me the peace of mind I needed to work and climb that corporate ladder to middle management. I had no further ambition at this point. I was good here. In fact, there were days I could go back to just a worker bee and not have the department's weight on my shoulders.

The day I learned about her passing; I felt the walls come down around me. I would let no one else in, and those that were got pushed out. That is, except for a select few, but I didn't want to be in this pain. I was numb for days, weeks, months, and I was starting to think I still was.

That's why I needed to do this. I needed to focus on something exciting. My grandmother would be cheering me on as well as laughing at me.

I could almost hear her voice say, "Treasure hunting, Amy, really? You have always been an adventurous soul."

"It's because you always had my back." I whispered to the air.

"Who are you talking to?" Scott stuck his head in the dining room where I was setting up for the video call with my girlfriends.

"Oh, just myself." I laughed. Why did he always have to get involved?

"So, you're really going to try this?" He came to put his hand on my shoulder.

"Yeah, if nothing else, it will be a fun trip with my friends. I haven't seen them since before you and I got married." Four years ago. I couldn't believe it had been four years since we got married.

"That was a good day." He leaned down to kiss me. "I think it's awesome you want to take this trip. You've been so moody and dramatic lately. This will be a good break."

My insides twisted. I knew he probably meant that differently than how it came out, but I couldn't help myself. I had to say something.

"Moody and dramatic? A nice break? A nice break from what? Us?"

"See? I say something, trying to be supportive and you twist it around. I support you. I love you. I want you to be happy." He threw his hands up in exasperation.

"But you couldn't think of another way than to insult me by saying I'm moody and dramatic?"

"Again, you are making my point for me."

My computer sounded that someone had logged into the call. It took our focus off the impending fight as we both looked angrily at my computer.

"I will let you get to that, but please know I love you and just said an innocent, idiotic thing." He kissed my head before leaving the room.

I groaned quietly as I threw my head back.

"1... 2... 3..." I counted softly to calm myself, then I smiled as I joined the call myself.

"Amy!" Heather squealed with delight as I joined.

"Hey, girl. How's it going?"

"Good, good. Lonely and quiet here, but good." A painful smile appeared on her face. I could tell she was trying to be brave.

"Aw, I understand. It gets quiet around here too. I miss the kids' sounds."

Another face popped on the screen.

"Hey, Denise!" Heather and I said in near unison, then laughed.

"Hey, ladies. So good to see you both."

"It's been too long." I said.

"It really has." Denise said.

Then our last guest appeared.

"Hey, my bitches!" She laughed.

"Ha! Welcome, Queen bitch." I laughed with her.

Heather pursed her lips. I don't know if I ever heard her say a curse word. Maybe we should have toned it down for her, but honestly, I was excited. Denise didn't bat an eye at the word as she laughed with us.

We spent a few minutes doing the usual round robin style catch up. What the kids were all up to, how our jobs were going, which unfortunately left poor Heather out. Her face fell a little as that topic was brought up. I don't know if the others noticed, but I did and so I quickly changed it as soon as the opportunity came around.

"Well, so the reason I wanted to chat was a little more than catching up, which I love doing, but...." I paused for the dramatic effect. Maybe Scott was on to something about being dramatic.

"You're pregnant!" Marissa blurted out with a chuckle.

"Curse you. NO!" I said. "I wanted to propose a girls' trip for us."

"That sounds much better than a baby at our age." Denise said.

"Unless it's a grandbaby." Heather smiled at me, knowing I was going to be a grandmother in just a few months.

"So, give us the deets. What's the trip?" Marissa asked.

"Alright so hear me out." I explained to them about the treasure hunting book and website. "Sooo, I thought we could do that."

"Are you serious?" Marissa asked with a nervous chuckle. "A treasure hunt?"

"It sounds fun to me," Heather giggled.

"Is it a very physical thing?" Denise asked.

She and I were the largest members of our group, at around 200 pounds each. Of course, her taller frame made her look more proportionate than me. At five-five, I was an apple with legs. Marissa was model thin with the stunning looks to match. While Heather had more of a mom's body, but was thin.

"I honestly don't know, but I think it has more to do with figuring out the clues than anything physical like climbing or diving or something." At least I hoped. I could walk a mile or so, but then I would want a break.

"I think we should do it." Heather said.

"I'm in." Denise said.

"Ya know, this all sounds crazy, but I'm in. I need a break." Marissa said.

"Alright! That's awesome."

"So, where do we start?"

"Fort Aston, Florida." I then told them about the first couple of clues that had already been solved and were now public knowledge. Then I filled them in on the homes I'd found. "I was thinking it made sense to stay in a house rather than a hotel."

"Yeah, hotels can get really loud."

"A house sounds like a perfect choice!"

"Love it."

"We just need to decide two things right now. When do we go and what will our team's name be?" I asked.

"Well, I can get away most anytime. I have nothing going on," Heather said.

Was it my imagination or did her voice crack? I raised an eyebrow to study her for a second. She smiled.

"I'm the boss, so as long as I don't have any client meetings, I'm free most anytime. I've hired good people," Marissa said, interrupting my train of thought on Heather's body language.

"Great! I think I can get away in a few weeks. We are wrapping on a project, and it will be live in production in three weeks and then I should be free." I offered.

"Yeah, I think three or four weeks from now works for me as well." Denise said.

"That will give us time to get ready and plan everything out." Heather added.

"We all know how you love to plan." I teased. The group laughed.

"Yeah, I can't help it." Heather chuckled. Glad she didn't take it personally.

"And it is one of the many things we love about you." Marissa added.

"Alright, so let's pick the house. Let me share what I'm looking at." I clicked the icon to share my desktop, then I pulled up the property management site. "Alright, this first one is my personal favorite. It is right across from a private resident only beach on a private street. It has a pool, a bar in the living room, and four bedrooms."

I flipped slowly through each picture, then read the amenities.

"Thoughts?" I asked.

"I love it."

"It's gorgeous."

"I see right where I'm going to have my coffee each morning."

"On that deck." We all said in almost unison, then laughed.

"Yeah. Right on that deck staring at the gulf." Denise said.

"So, do we even look at the others?" I asked.

"I don't think we need to."

"I'm good with this one.

"Nope, no need to look. That's our place."

Decision one made.

"Alright dates."

We chatted around trying to narrow it down, settling on dates in exactly four weeks from today.

"Now a team name. Then we can register on the website."

"It's simple." Heather said. "Treasure Hunting Mamas!"

"Ohmygosh, that's perfect."

"Love it."

"Clever!"

"So, we agree. That's the name?"

"Yes."

I pulled up the registration form on the website and began filling it in. I had to put all our email addresses in it. When I hit submit, a compass popped up and began spinning, indicating our application was processing.

"Wow, this is exciting." Heather clapped.

"Oh, there it is... Congratulations, your team has been accepted. Happy hunting." I read the message out loud. It also said we each should have gotten an email with a confirmation link in it.

"Got mine."

"Me too."

"Same. I clicked it."

"So, is that it?"

"That's it." I smiled. "Now we just need to prep and get ready for the trip! I'm going to send you each a copy of the book, so between the book and the website, we can start thinking about the clues. Well, it is just one clue that we are supposed to find in a church there. It is known for its intricate stained-glass windows. The next clue is in one of those windows, or at least that's the current rumor. We'll need to review it to decide if we agree."

Everyone agreed.

"I can't wait to pack," Heather said.

"How many lists are you going to make?" I teased her.

"Ha, ha, but probably five." She chuckled softly.

With that out and plans in motion, we said good night, agreeing to touch base regularly as we got ready for the trip. We ended the call.

I smiled as my screen went back to my desktop wallpaper. It was a picture of my four children from Aiden's high school graduation just two years ago. They humored me by letting me take a picture of them.

Then I ordered each of the ladies a copy of the book, shipping it directly to each of them. With the two-day shipping, it should give them plenty of time to read the book before our trip.

I shut down the computer, then went to join Scott in the living room. He was working on his laptop, but looked up when I came in.

"How'd it go?"

"Good. Everyone's on board."

"That's great. I'm excited for you."

"Yeah, you'll be okay with me going?"

"Of course. When?"

I filled him on the dates.

"Oh, wow, that's quick, but I'm happy for you." He smiled and then turned back to his work.

"You still have that big presentation tomorrow?"

"Yeah, I'm just trying to review everything once more."

I picked up my eReader. "I'll just read and be quiet so you can focus."

He simply looked over and smiled, then turned back to it.

It always felt like we were walking on eggshells. I could tell he was being careful with his words. I understood. My temper had been shorter lately. Hormones and depression, stress from work, it all added up to me being, what were his words, moody and dramatic. He wasn't wrong about that.

I looked over my device at him, trying not to stare too much or catch his attention. I did love that man. No matter how frustrated I got at times, I couldn't picture life without him.

Conflicted with my thoughts, I went back to my reader and try not to think about life, if only for a few minutes.

Chapter Six: Heather

Jason got home around seven. I had been fidgeting with excitement since I got off the call with my friends.

This was all so exciting. I couldn't wait to tell him about the trip. I know he would be happy for me.

He walked in the doors looking hollow and stressed, but his eye lit up when he saw me.

"Hey." He pulled me to him, kissing me.

"Hey, yourself." I mumbled as the kiss ended. "Long day?"

"Oh, so long. I'm sorry that I work so much. I'm hoping things will slow once this merger is complete. All this reorganization to make two companies into one has really taken its toll on, well, everyone."

"Are you hungry? Did you get any supper?"

"Yeah, they brought in dinner so we could focus." His face changed as a wicked smile crossed his face. "But I could use some dessert."

He pulled me to him, kissing me again, and letting his hands explore.

I giggled and murmured his name.

An hour later, we were fresh out of the shower and holding hands on the couch in front of the television. I don't even know what was on. Some history thing he was into.

I hadn't even gotten to tell him about my day yet, but I waited until a commercial.

"I talked to Amy, Marissa, and Denise earlier."

"Oh, yeah, anything good?"

"Actually, yes. We are planning a girls' trip."

"Fun, you love those. Where are y'all thinking of going?"

"Florida. A place called Fort Aston."

"Wait? Seriously?"

"Have you heard of it?"

"That's what this show is about. They're talking about a treasure hunt and that is where one treasure is supposedly buried."

"This show right now?" I had been so lost in my own thoughts; I hadn't been paying attention at all.

"Yeah, this one."

"Amy was telling us about it and, in fact," I hesitated because it sounded silly as I started to say it. "That's why we are going to look for that treasure."

"Seriously, that's so cool. I know a little bit about it. I can help."

"I would love to hear what you know about it. Amy said she was sending us each the book, and we registered on the website."

"You have access to the website?"

"I do. Do you want to see it?"

"Um, yeah!"

I pulled it up on my phone, and we clicked through some screens, then handed him the phone so he could browse through the forums.

"See, here is the one for the Fort Aston treasure. The story here is about a man, last name Aston. He was an officer in the early US Navy. He was commissioned to fight pirates in the Florida Gulf Coast from Tampa Bay all the way to the Pensacola area."

He told me about how there was a great battle between the most notorious pirate Captain Claude de Palencia. He had been the largest threat and was hung after he was captured.

"It is a really interesting story, much more than the tidbits I'm giving you."

"I can't wait to get the book so I can read it myself."

The show came back on and this time, I paid attention. They started in on the first clue.

The town's namesake was a skilled seaman, took on the pirates in battle after battle, winning all but the one.

"Wait? He didn't win one." I blurted.

"Yes, that's right. Captain de Palencia was captured, as were many of the crew, but those that weren't came after Commodore Aston and assassinated him."

"Wow." This show was getting me even more excited about this trip. I was hooked on the story.

After it ended, we went to bed, but I couldn't sleep. I laid awake thinking about the Commodore, the pirate, the church clue.

In the sea in the ship to the left of the south and the song to the west. It shows the way to the end, to the victory.

It had to mean east, but east of what? The victory was winning the battle, but it wasn't the end since the men came after him later. Still, where had the battle taken place? At sea? I hoped we didn't have to snorkel. I was claustrophobic, so I had never had luck with snorkeling.

Ah, well, I wouldn't solve it tonight and in the year that people have been searching for this, nobody had found it yet. Little ole me would not solve it in a few hours.

I settled under the covers and stared at the bedroom curtains, the beige floral ones I had sown years ago when my boys were little. Perhaps it was time to make over our bedroom. I could sew new curtains, change the pictures on the walls. I lifted my head slightly to look at my favorite landscaped print hanging across the room.

Maybe I can keep that one. I thought.

Then I thought of the boys' rooms. Tyler's was the only one that we had changed since we knew he wasn't coming home. He had an apartment with two roommates, and a part-time job to pay for it while he continued on with school.

Cody was still a question mark, but with each day, it looked like he wasn't coming home. Especially now that he had a paid internship lined up for this summer and he lived on campus the rest of the time. Perhaps it was time we downsized the house.

The thought made me sad. My babies were born and lived their entire lives here. This is where all my memories of those years took place. No, I wasn't ready, so I wouldn't bring it up to Jason.

The next day, I woke up before Jason and, like most days; I started the coffee and then I waited. I waited to find my purpose in this new chapter of my life.

A lightbulb went off in my mind.

The trip.

It would be the perfect distraction to get me over this funk. The coffee pot stopped, so I poured a mug full, grabbed my laptop, and went to the living room. My favorite spot for being on the computer. I could have the television on for the noise and the olive-green microfiber couch was soft and comfy. There was an end table on each side of the couch, so I could put my mug down as I needed, but for now I held the warm mug, smelling in the bitter coffee smell. It was comforting.

I snuggled against the cushioned back, then grabbed the remote to turn on the television, flipping until I found a home improvement show.

"Perfect."

I took a sip of the coffee, then set it down, pulling up the treasure site on my computer. I headed straight to the message boards, pulling up the one for Fort Aston. Amy had already told us, but the show confirmed that this was only one of ten treasures that had been hidden across the United States.

I didn't bother to look at those, but maybe if we found this one, we could find others. I smiled at the thought. Treasure hunting could be my new purpose.

I heard a curse from our room, causing me to cringe. He must have overslept. I should have woken him up, but I didn't know what time he had to get up.

I listened to him rushing around our room as he got ready. I put the computer to the side and went to fix his coffee. Pulling out his travel mug, I filled it and then grabbed the power bar he liked, placing it next to the cup.

"Oh, my gosh." He said, coming in. "I can't believe I overslept. I should have asked you to wake me."

"I'm sorry. I should have thought of it." I handed him the mug and bar. He smiled.

"Nope, not your fault. I'm a big boy." He took the items from me.

"That you are." I said playfully.

"Watch out, Mrs. Connolly, or I might just call in sick to show you." He pulled me to him with his free hand, giving me a toe-curling kiss. When it ended, he smiled at me. "Thanks for the coffee. I'll try to be home earlier tonight, okay?"

"Okay. Have a good one, babe."

"You too."

Then he was gone, and the house felt empty. I couldn't even explain the hollow feeling. The silence would have been deafening, except for the television being on. I walked through the first floor of the house, looking around.

"Maybe it was time to downsize." I grumbled to myself.

This really was too much house for two people. Moving would give me a project to work on, at least short term. Maybe after the trip, I could talk to Jason about it to get his thoughts, but no point thinking too much until after that.

I went back to reading through the forums. There were a dozen or so other teams registered to look for the Fort Aston treasure, like us, but at current it didn't seem like anyone was there actively searching.

I spent an hour doing that. After that, I started doing research on the city. I started my first list: places to eat. There were a lot of fun options. With us staying in a house, we could cook some meals there, especially breakfasts. Depending on how the treasure hunting was going and what other activities we would do that day would depend on where we would eat.

After making a list, I looked up the church. Just as Amy had said, it was famous for its windows. They had public tours daily, except Sundays, or if there was a private event. All those dates were posted.

People came from all over the world to see them. The website for the church warned to plan for crowds and that earlier in the day was better than the afternoon.

"Noted." I said, as I wrote it on my next list: Things to do.

This was part of the treasure hunt, but I still added it to the list of things we would be doing. There was the actual Fort Aston as well. I bet a clue was there, maybe two. Even if there wasn't, I wanted to see the fort. It is where the Commodore was killed. There was a ghost tour. People claimed it was haunted by his ghost. I don't know if I believe that, but the history of the fort interested me.

The ladies would want to spend time in the pool or beach. Neither was of that much interest to me. I had a pool now that I rarely got in. We had it built for the boys. Now they weren't home to use it.

I looked at the living room windows to the sparkling blue water. The aqua and teal tiles around the pool were beautiful. I had fallen in love with them at first sight.

I should put on my swimsuit and float around in the pool. That would be nice.

"Yes, I'm going to do it."

I closed the laptop, putting on one of the end tables, then went to change. After I was changed, I grabbed a towel and then a couple of the pool noodles from the garage. I tested the water with my toe. A bit cold, but the day was warm and with the sun out, it should be fine.

I threw the noodles in and then dove into myself, swimming a few laps, stretching my old swimming muscles. Then I rounded up the pool noodles, I positioned myself so I could lie out and float around.

Closing my eyes, I daydreamed about a pool near the beach with a fruit drink in one hand and my friends floating around nearby. We would laugh as we chatted about this or that. Nothing serious. It would be nice not to be alone for nearly every minute of every day. Doing nothing as I waited for something magical to happen.

I giggled as I continued my float and continued my daydream about the upcoming trip. This was going to be a fun distraction.

Chapter Seven: Marissa

After I hung up with my friends, I stared at the screen for a minute, processing the conversation. This offered me a much needed, much deserved break from my life. Between the pressures at work and at home, I always felt on, always moving and doing, but rarely for me.

I mean, the company was mine, but it had grown so quickly that I still couldn't believe it was real. It had just been my process for working at my tiny, barely $30k a year HR Assistant job when I was a newlywed.

A manager heard how I organized myself and our work projects, asking me to do a demonstration for him from start to finish. He promoted me on the spot to a Project Manager asking me to revamp the processes for the entire Human Resources department. Then he put me in touch with our IT department. They helped automate the processes.

After a year, the manager suggested I quit to start it as a full company.

"You are incredibly smart, Marissa. You should take this and run with it."

"But I wouldn't have gotten here without you believing in me."

"Yeah, but I think even without me, you would have gotten here. I just... believed in you." He smiled.

"Come with me."

"No, just promise you will remember me when you are famous."

"Famous? From a dinky little software program." I laughed, but now that conversation seemed so foretelling. I wouldn't go so far as to say famous, but with over eighty companies using our product now, I was known.

A few magazines had done an article on me as an up-and-coming executive, which got me a few stares when in public.

Olivia came bouncing down the stairs.

"Bye, mom!" She waved as she headed for the front door.

"Whoa, hold up. Where are you going?"

"Out with friends."

"Did you ask?"

"I asked dad."

"Well, he didn't tell me. Let's go ask him."

"Mom, no. My friends are here."

"Where? Nobody knocked on the door."

"They texted from the car."

"That's how this is done. They come to the door. I get eyes on who is driving my baby girl around for the night and you ask me to go out. Dad's not in charge."

"But he is a parent."

"Yeah, but he doesn't always know what's going on."

We found Mike in the office as he was reading something on his computer. He looked up, eyes glossed over, which meant he was in work mode, not dad or husband mode. If she had asked him, he hadn't heard her at all and just reactively answered her.

"What's up?" He asked.

"Did you tell Olivia she could go out tonight?"

"No."

"Dad, I just came in here and asked."

"Did you? I'm sorry. I didn't hear you. I'm reading this brief from work."

"It's Friday night. Why are you working?" Olivia fumed.

"Because grown-ups have a lot of responsibilities."

"Ugh, so can I go or what?"

"Who is driving?" I asked.

"Jade."

"Who else is going?" I continued.

She rolled her eyes. "Ava and Paige. And before you ask, we are going to the mall. We are planning to eat something in the food court, do some window shopping, and then go to the movies. I will be home at 1 am because of when the movie gets out."

"Fine. I'll walk you out." I smiled at Mike over my shoulder, but he had gotten back to work.

I know sometimes he didn't feel like he gave us enough or did enough for us because of my job. It was a conversation we have had several times. He was a defense attorney, so his job was probably even more important than mine. I always tried to tell him how proud I was of him. He worked hard, too hard at times, trying to overcompensate for his perceived shortfalls.

It made me want to quit my job to help take the self-imposed pressure off of him.

But, honestly, I was just as bad about overcompensating. I did too much for everyone to try to prove that I could do it all, handle it all, but I was burning myself out.

We stepped outside, and I saw Jade's sporty car at the curb. The girls in it all looked around at each other as I walked towards them.

"Sorry." Olivia mumbled as she got inside.

"Evenin', ladies. Just wanted to say hi before you all take off for the evening. Olivia told me your plans for the evening. It sounds fun."

"Yeah, we have been waiting for this concert for months." Ava said.

"Ava!" Olivia snapped.

"What?"

"Yeah, that's what I thought. Out, Liv."

"Damn it." She pushed open the door hard, climbing out. "You're ruining my life." She stormed into the house.

"I hope the rest of you told your parents the truth about where exactly you are going. Not like my daughter. Now she will be grounded, and I'll have her phone. Keep that in mind before snapping, tweeting, or whatever you kids are doing these days. Have a good night." I turned and went to deal with my lying teen.

Not that I was perfect as a teen. I lied to my parents anytime I thought they would say no. It wasn't until years later that I learned they would have said yes, a lot more had I just been honest.

"What's going on?" Mike said, coming from the office.

He was now in dad mode. Thank goodness, because I wasn't ready to deal with Olivia by myself. I was already concerned she would sneak out to meet up with her friends.

"She lied about where they were going tonight."

"Really?" Mike looked up the stairs to the kids' rooms. "Should I go talk to her?"

"No, it should be me." I looked up the stairs. "But maybe you could come with me for backup."

Thirty minutes later, I had all her electronic devices, and she was crying on her floor. I felt bad, in some ways, but lies had consequences. Period. She had to learn that. I was raising them to be adults, not raising them to remain children.

"Thanks for the backup." I said to Mike as we walked back downstairs. I needed to get dinner on the table. Mom and dad had medications to take with food, so they would need to eat.

"Always. Want me to order something in? It will free you up and you can just have a glass of wine or something."

"Oh, my gosh, that would be wonderful. Thank you."

"Pizza sound, okay? Everyone loves pizza, right?"

"That works for me." I headed for the kitchen and a bottle of wine.

Mom and dad were sitting at the table doing a crossword together. They looked up when I came into the room.

"Oh, hi, Mike is going to order pizza."

"I love pizza. I better make sure he gets it from Tony's and not from one of those chains." Dad said and stood to go find Mike.

My dad had nothing against the chain of restaurants, but he loved to support local businesses. He often said if not for his own small business, he couldn't have put me through college.

I got my wine and brought mom a juice, then sat next to her. I wanted to vent to her about Olivia, but if she wasn't completely mom right now, I didn't want to confuse her.

"Teenagers. What are you going to do?" Mom laughed softly.

"Yeah, sorry for all the trouble I caused you as a teen." I reached for her hand. Happy to hear she was my mother in this moment.

"Oh, darlin', you were a piece of cake compared to yours, but I appreciate the apology."

"Where did I go wrong?"

"She's just strong-willed. It means she's going to go far, if you don't kill her before then."

"Thanks, mom."

Ella came down to join us. She didn't say a word about her sister. I'm sure she already knew. She started doing the crossword with her grandmother. A few minutes later, Jackson came down.

"Where's dinner?"

"On the way. Dad ordered pizza."

"Dang it. Okay, can you call me when it's here?" He turned to leave.

"Whoa, stop. How about you join us for conversation and companionship here?" I smiled.

"Mom, why are you so clingy? I have a paper due and I'm nearly done with it, but I thought it was dinnertime." He pointed to the clock.

"Well, I'm sorry it's late. Should be any second, so why not have a seat here with us and wait?"

He rolled his eyes.

"Jack, sit down like your mother said. Someday she may not be here and you'll be sorry then." Mom said firmly, but lovingly. She rarely talked to anyone like that these days, so it shocked all of us.

"Yes, ma'am." He frowned and sat.

"That's better. Now, how is school going?" Mom asked him.

"Great. Just extremely busy, with it being nearly the end of this semester."

"Grades are good?"

"Yes, grandma."

"That's good. Now, is this so bad to sit and talk?"

He looked at her with a grin, his face relaxed. "Yeah, it's not so bad."

"Pizza's here." Dad announced as he followed Mike into the kitchen.

Mike was the one carrying all the pizza boxes.

"Thanks, Lenny. I could have said that," Mike said as he slid them onto our kitchen island.

I hopped up to grab plates. Everyone grabbed a slice or two, or in Jackson and Mike's cases, they each got four. Olivia shuffled in, but kept her face down. She grabbed a plate and one slice of pizza, then sat on a bar stool away from the table.

"You can sit with us." I said.

"I'm not talking to you."

"You lied to me, and I'm still talking to you. Now, come sit with your family. Look, even your brother is here."

"Fine." She stomped her foot, then collapsed into a chair. "Happy?"

"Yes. Thank you."

As we ate, Mike, Jackson and dad chatted about video games. I don't know when my dad got so into gaming, but he was hooked. It might be because when Mike wasn't working, he was playing some game or another.

Jackson would sometimes make a rare appearance to join them, especially last month when a new game they had been looking forward to came out. It was the three of them in the den, gaming and yelling for hours. I just sent in food and drinks, and ran the girls around.

Jackson helped himself to another couple of slices. I didn't complain he was eating with us, laughing, talking. It was nice. If he asked for money or a new car at the end of this, I might just give it to him. He caught me looking at him and he smiled. It was a genuine, beautiful Jackson smile for his mom.

After dinner, he took the trash out and offered to walk the block with his grandparents. They always took a stroll after dinner. Olivia and Ella joined them.

"Who is that kid?" Mike asked once they were gone.

"Mom yelled at him. Ella was here so I'm sure she is being careful to stay on grandma's good side."

"Well, go Sandra." He chuckled. "I love your mom, you know."

"Yes, I know. I sometimes think you only asked me to marry you because of them."

"It's true." He pulled me into his lap, kissing me softly. "But it helps that I fell in love with you, too."

"Smooth talker, that's what I fell in love with."

He laughed.

"So, with everyone gone, I wanted to talk to you about something." I said.

"Sounds serious."

"No, nothing too serious. You know I had that call with the girls earlier."

"Oh, yeah, how'd that go?"

"Well, that's the thing. Amy proposed a girls' trip to Florida. I said I'd go, but I probably should have at least talked to you first." I bite my lip. Not normally the submissive type, but at that moment, I felt it a bit. Sitting in his lap, realizing I should have talked to him out of respect. He would have to pick up my slack around here, and that wasn't something he shined at.

"No, you don't have to talk to me, well, I mean I guess..." He studied me. "We have a good thing here, babe. If you think you can do it with work, then all I need to know is when." He smiled.

"In four weeks."

"Okay. Put it on the board." He mocked me.

"Ha. Yes, sir." I saluted and tried to stand up to follow his order, but he held me in his lap.

"I wasn't done with you yet."

I giggled in his lap as he started kissing me again.

Chapter Eight: Denise

I looked around my empty apartment. Nobody here to talk to. Nobody here to check my vacation with. I laughed.

After all the abuse, lies, and manipulation during the three years with Sid's father, I had no interest in starting a relationship with anyone. I loved being single.

The vacation sounded like so much fun. Of course, I'd have to talk with my doctor to make sure it wouldn't interfere with treatments. My surgery had been scheduled, but it wasn't for two months. We would be back by then, hopefully with treasure in hand and a lot of fun memories.

My plan was to take a lot of pictures so I could look at them while doing my chemo or when recovery from surgery. Good memories instead of whatever hell I would endure soon.

Since I had good luck with the baby forums when I had Sidney, I pulled up the ones I found for cancer. I had yet to post anything, but I loved reading the stories of survival and hope. I spent an hour reading through a man's journey from discovery to remission.

"Wow, this sounds like where I am now." As I read his first few entries. It took most of the evening, but I got to the end of his journey to remission. "I hope this is how my journey goes, too."

I pushed the computer away and headed to the kitchen to find something for dinner. At the store yesterday, I'd picked up a lot more quick, easy, yet healthy options. Fresh veggies, lean meats, and things to make a few low-fat, homemade dressings.

I pulled out some lettuce and other veggies to throw together a salad. I had already mixed up a ginger sesame dressing so that it would be ready to go. I took my dinner into the living room so I could watch TV while I ate.

"Okay, this isn't half bad." I mumbled to myself when I was about halfway through it.

I could have been doing this all along, but I was stupid and lazy, using being busy as an excuse. But the prep took only a few minutes and if I planned ahead, I could have all the vegetables cleaned and cut up, ready to go at a minute's notice.

I set it on the coffee table when I was done and then snuggled into my favorite throw blanket to watch television. I dozed off, waking a few hours later to darkness outside and only the television for light. Turning it off as I pushed up, grabbing my bowl from dinner, taking it to the kitchen to wash it. Then headed to bed.

I woke late the next morning. Checking the time, I needed to get moving. I had gotten invited to a baby shower for a co-worker, Brooke. She was probably the closest friend I had locally. We joked we were each other's work wife, but the truth was it was more like mother-daughter as I was the same age as her mother.

Despite that, I wouldn't tell her anything that was going on as she would soon have a little boy to bond with and that needed to be her complete focus. Hopefully she would be on maternity leave for the worst of my treatments and would never need to know.

I pulled out a new sundress and sandals I'd bought for today. It fit perfectly over my extra curves, hiding my many sins. I slipped on the sandals and then look at myself in the full-length mirror.

"Not bad. Could be better." I pinched at a fat roll. If I got to remission, I promised myself that I'd do better.

I ran a brush through my hair. It had been board straight since the day I was born and so there wasn't much I could do with it, anyway. A little mascara and tinted lip gloss, and I was ready to go.

I grabbed the gift bag with the little baby holding a balloon and overflowing with blue tissue paper from the kitchen counter, then picked up my keys and purse.

In the car, I turned up the music as loud as I could stand it. I didn't want to think about doctors or cancer. I just wanted to sing 80s music and then go celebrate my friend's new baby.

But I couldn't help it, my mind kept thinking about it. It was going to be strange to do this normal thing today when I knew this bad thing was in me right now. I felt vulnerable as if everyone that looked my way would know.

It was a silly thought, but I couldn't help feeling that way. My doctor had said it was important to do normal things and not stop living my life. She was an amazing doctor.

I pulled up about ten minutes later. I'd promised her I would come to help, which meant I was one of the first guests to arrive. The other two were her mother and sister.

"Knock, knock." I said, stepping in. Brooke's house had an open-door policy, especially today.

"Hey! Come in." Her sister, Kayla said. "Brooke should be ready in a sec. Mom brought her a new dress for today, so she went to change."

"Okay." I set the gift down on a table near the door. "What can I do to help?"

"Can you help me with balloons? I have a helium tank and I just need help tying the ribbons as I blow them up."

"Alright."

She started blowing up the balloons, then would pass it off to me. I tied the long, curling ribbons on and then took the next one from her. We were able to get three done before Brooke and her mother, Chrissy, came out of Brooke's room.

"Oh, Brooke, you look gorgeous!" Kayla said as she passed me another balloon.

"Yes, you are glowing." I smiled.

Chrissy smiled at me. I'd met her several times in the past. She was a sweet lady and so excited to be a grandmother soon.

"I'm sweating from every pore. I feel like I'm literally cooking this baby." She laughed. "I'm so glad you made it." She came over and hugged me.

"Of course, I would come. I have to celebrate this little guy." I touched her belly.

I wouldn't do that with someone I didn't know, but after I found Brooke laying on the bathroom floor at work, unable to stop throwing up, we formed an even stronger bond. She had the worst morning sickness, and I had thought mine was bad with Sidney.

At least mine had gotten better after a few hours. Poor Brooke had been sick morning, noon, and night until about a month ago. She only had two more months until baby boy Larkin was welcomed into the world.

We finished getting the balloons done and then set out all the food. We finished as the first few guests arrived. Within about a fifteen minute period, all the guests arrived.

I knew only a few of them, so those of us that worked with Brooke sat together, clinging to familiar people. Though I did branch out a little when Kayla or Brooke pulled me in to help them pass out clothespins for our first game.

"Tell them they have to pin this to their shirt and then, during the party, if anyone says baby, they take their pin. The person with the most at the end wins."

"Got it."

Immediately after passing them out, you could see that her family was a competitive bunch. They were all trying really hard to get others to say the taboo word.

"Thank you for coming today to celebrate Brooke's... umm... at the... umm." One of Brooke's aunts, Stacy, was saying.

"Baby shower?" The unsuspecting guest offered.

"Got ya," Stacy said, holding her hand out for the other guest's pin.

"Oh, darn. You're good. I'm going to keep an eye on you."

I would have to remember that trick.

An hour later, food had been eaten, pins had transferred around, and we were ready for another game.

"Okay, for this game, I'm going to need to suspend the pin game for a short time because there is no way we can get through it without saying the word... Good?"

Everyone agreed.

"Alright, so Brooke and Jayden have kept the name a secret until today. Baby Boy Larkin will be..." Kayla turned to Brooke.

"Jasper Brook Larkin." She smiled.

"Seriously?" Chrissy blurted out. "My grandson's name will be Jasper?"

There was a gasp from the room. Brooke started crying.

"See? This is why I have kept it a secret. You always do this." She ran off to her room.

We all looked around, almost holding our collective breaths. The only sound was the tick of the wall clock. Kayla aggressively pointed to her mother to join her in the kitchen. Despite being in another room, their conversation could still be heard by all the guests.

"That was extremely rude and uncalled for. That is going to be your grandson. Your *first* grandson."

"Well, I don't like it and she should know now before he is born."

"Mom, it is her and Jayden's decision, not yours."

"The world is hard enough on kids without giving them a name that can lead to teasing and bullying."

"Why do you automatically think that?"

"Because I watch the news."

"Oh, yeah? Well, I'm a teacher. I see all the kids' names and they are all as unique as each child. Nobody really cares what the name is. They mostly accept each other. If someone is a bully, they will find another reason to pick on the other child. They can even have the same name."

"Hmph, whatever, I don't like it."

"Well, guess what? They do like it, and he is their baby. And for the record, I love it and already love Jasper very much. I can't wait to be his aunt."

Kayla suddenly came through the room and down the short hall to Brooke's bedroom. We all looked around at each other as we sat in polite, awkward silence.

Chrissy didn't come out of the kitchen for a minute or two, but when she did, she simply came out and sat back in her chair. Her face was red, but she offered an embarrassed smile.

Kayla and Brooke came back.

"I'm sorry. Just a bit hormonal from being pregnant." Brooke smiled, wiping tears from her cheeks. "So, the game is we have these papers, and you try to come up with as many words as you can from his name." She looked at her mother.

"That sounds fun," Chrissy offered, in lieu of an apology.

They started passing out the pages, and we were given five minutes to come up with as many words as we could.

"And, begin!"

Pens started flying across paper as everyone started with a few easy ones like book, park, kin, and spin. Well, those were the first ones I wrote. I got about a dozen or so written down, but then my brain couldn't think of anymore. I looked around and several others were looking up, too. We smiled at each other and then looked over at those still writing.

I studied the words again, trying to think of more, but nothing.

"Okay, time." Kayla said.

A mix of groans and laughs at the ending of the game. The counting began.

"Okay, if you think you have the most, raise your hand."

I knew I didn't as I barely got fifteen and I could see that others had far more. A few hands went up, including our co-worker, Janis.

When Kayla pointed to her, she announced her number.

"22."

Several hands went down. I guess twenty-two was a good number.

A cousin, Libby, announced she had gotten the same.

"Great minds." Libby said as they leaned towards each other to compare their lists.

"Some overlap, but some not." They laughed.

"Okay, then the number to beat twenty-two. Anyone with better?"

"I have… um… 27!" Sarah said. She was one of Brooke's childhood friends.

All eyes in the room looked over with awe.

"Anyone beat 27?" Kayla glanced around.

"I have 55." Another cousin, Aimee announced.

"Wow. Anyone with more?" She looked around as heads shook no. "Alright, Aimee, you're the winner!"

She handed Aimee a small gift bag that was stuffed with scented hand lotion, soaps, and bath bombs.

They moved on to another game. I mostly went through the motions as my stomach felt a little upset. Oh, boy, could I just get through this party without issues? I willed my stomach to calm down until the end.

That vulnerable feeling crept up on me again. It felt as if I had the word cancer flashing above my head. If I got sick now, it would be even more noticeable.

Luckily, it listened, and I got through without having any issues. I was even able to help with the cleanup, which gave me a little time to talk to Brooke.

"You got some lovely gifts."

"Yes, I did. I can't wait to get to dress him and watch him enjoy the toys."

"I'm excited for you."

"Thanks so much for coming. It means a lot that you were here." She hugged me. "You feeling okay?"

"Oh, yeah, why?" Uh-oh, was it obvious? Had the word cancer been tattooed on my face? I knew it hadn't, but it almost felt like it.

"You just look tired." The concern in her voice had me feeling guilty.

"Nothing a good nap won't solve. I'll get out of here, but thanks for having me."

With that, I headed home and straight to for bed. It had been a good day, and I wanted to hold on to those fun memories in the coming months.

Chapter Nine: Amy

It was only two weeks until the trip. Each time I thought about it, I did a little happy dance. This was going to be fun, and a much needed break from life.

Scott had been extremely supportive when I'd told him about the trip.

"I think it sounds like a wonderful idea."

"You do?" I don't know why I was surprised, but I was.

"Yeah. You haven't been yourself lately and I think you could use some time away."

"Haven't been myself? What do you mean?"

"Just that you've seemed, I don't know, almost depressed."

"Depressed? That's absurd." I tried to laugh, but my mind knew it was the truth.

I had thought the same thing a few times, but I wouldn't admit it to him. It felt like a weakness, and after being in two failed marriages, I didn't want to show any vulnerability.

I studied him.

I really should treat Scott as a new person, not as if he was one of my exes, but I couldn't help myself. My marriage to Carlos had been volatile.

He mostly wanted a son which he got. Once Aiden was born, Carlos filed for divorce and then fought hard for custody. After a year of mediation and courtroom drama, we settled on a fifty-fifty split custody.

I had only been divorced from Carlos a few months when I'd met Scott. I probably wasn't in the right frame of mind for a relationship.

It was probably stupid to get right into a relationship before the dust had settled on my divorce, but here I am now, five years later.

We had been happy in the beginning, and maybe we still were. I loved him, but the fighting was really wearing on me.

"Don't get defensive." He slipped his arms around me, kissing my forehead. "I promise, I support you and just want you to be happy."

"Okay." I smiled, but my guard was up. Up high.

That was two weeks ago, and I hadn't gotten over it, and is probably why the next few fights got so heated. We had a fight about who took the trash out last, followed by a big one that stemmed from cooking dinner.

"I have an hour of work left to do, and it's your turn," He snapped.

"I cooked last night, so it's *your turn.*"

"Why are you so bitchy?"

"Bitchy, oh buddy, you haven't even seen bitchy yet."

We ended up ordering pizza after an hour of screaming back and forth. He was awake until midnight finishing his work and I slept in the guest room. Nobody won, but the pizza was good, so I guess pizza won.

Each night, I read a few pages of Michael Carren's book about the treasure hunt, but only the section about the one we were trying to go for. I wanted to memorize the story of Commodore William Aston and Pirate Claude de Palencia. It would help with understanding and decoding the clues.

Also, after we'd registered our team, we had put in the known clues, so it progressed us along the hunt. We were tied with everyone else, with the next clue being in the St. Peter's Catholic Church in Fort Aston, Florida. It was where the Commodore and town namesake had been celebrated when he passed away.

The Commodore's story was interesting. His legacy was fighting and protecting the Gulf Coast area against pirates in the mid-1840s. It was right around the time that Florida became a part of the United States.

The famous Pirate Claude de Palencia was his biggest adversary. They were in a five-year battle, but Commodore Aston captured and hung the great pirate along with several crew members. The surviving men attacked the Commodore in his sleep, killing him. They were then captured and hung for their crime.

Only half his booty had ever been recovered and was rumored to be lost somewhere along the coast between Florida and Alabama.

That was not the hunt we were on. We were searching for the almost guaranteed treasure set up by Michael Carren.

"This is going to be exciting." I told Archie.

I was reading in our bedroom while Scott was in the office, working late.

"Did you say something, babe?" Scott said, poking his head in.

"Oh, sorry, just excited about this trip."

"I'm glad." He crossed the room, sitting next to me on the bed. "You're going to have so much fun."

"I hope so."

"Well, I better get back to work. Big presentation." He kissed my head, then left the room.

Setting the book aside, I flipped the television on, settling on the food channel. It would make perfect background noise. Then I grabbed my phone. I scrolled through the pictures of our rental house. It was gorgeous.

I can't wait! I thought.

Looking over at my sleeping cat, I wished I could take him with me, but I knew he probably wouldn't even know that I was gone. As long as his food was filled on time and his litter box cleaned out, he was a pretty happy cat.

My phone chimed. It was Heather messaging the group. She had started a list of everything we'd need, including the entire meal plan for the trip. Each day we would get a new list or idea or something from her.

I rolled my eyes and chuckled at my longtime friend. She'd had always been this way. Growing up, if I didn't have a pencil for class, Heather had extras. Need a tampon? Ask Heather. Every girls' trip, she had the itinerary memorized. I loved her so much.

I told her over and over that we would play the trip by ear based on the clues. This wasn't a regular vacation. We were at the mercy of where the clues took us.

This text was a link to a bar called Wild Flamingo's.

Heather: Karaoke and awesome looking drinks. We might need to take a treasure hunting break for this place.

Cool place. I replied.

Marissa replied with a thumb's up and Denise said she already had her karaoke song picked out.

I laughed, replying with a laughing face.

We continued to text back and forth with various things.

Denise: I'm so ready for this!

Heather: *squeal*

Marissa: So need a break

Denise: I need a new duffel bag for the trip

Heather: Is it too early to pack?

Marissa: I have a general plan of what I'll pack, but still time.

Me: I have no idea where my bags are

When I realized that, I nearly panicked but honestly, I had time if I needed to buy something. But let me go look for them now.

I hopped up to begin the hunt for my favorite duffel in our closet. It was a wheeled version that was perfect because I could cram half my closest into it. I was one of those classic over packers. The me that packed and the me on vacation were two different people.

"What are you doing?" Scott asked.

"I'm looking for my bag for the trip."

"And you have to do it right now?"

"Sorry, was I being too loud?" I wasn't even in the same room with him. A fight was on the horizon. I could just feel it.

"No, but it's distracting. I'm already behind on this project."

"That's not my fault!"

"Well, you aren't helping."

"Scott, before this blows up into a fight, I'm going to walk away. I'm in no mood for your attitude tonight."

That was all it took. Thirty minutes later, I was crying and stewing in the guest room with the cat while he was pounding out his frustrations on the treadmill.

He really ticked me off sometimes. Maybe my words had *a touch* of attitude, but I honestly meant I didn't want to fight tonight.

Tomorrow was a big day at work. We were rolling out a new major release of our software. This was an all-hands-on deck type of day so that we could get it done, tested, and signed off, with as little interruption to our users as possible.

I didn't need to be up stress crying about my marriage, fretting about every word we said to each other. My mind was already occupied by release notes and test scripts and packing lists and clues to a treasure.

"Damn you, Scott." I muttered as I flipped on the guest room's television.

Archie stretched and climbed on my chest, nuzzling my chin until I finally rubbed his chin and ears. Petting him relaxed me enough that I fell asleep.

The next morning, I woke to the alarm. I fought the urge to throw it across the room. The night had been as expected, fitful, many tears, and long. I had dozed off with Archie, but the first of many wake ups later, he had moved to the other side of the bed.

I headed first to the bathroom. My reflection looked old and haggard.

"Yikes!" I splashed water on my face, then headed for the coffeepot.

The house was quiet, which was strange. Scott was usually up and moving around by now. I took my coffee and headed down the hall to our room.

The door was open, and our bed was made. No Scott to be found.

Weird.

I went to his office. Laptop was gone. He must have already gone into work. Good, I could get dressed in peace. No surprise penis at every turn.

In the shower, I lingered a bit. The hot water felt good on my puffy face, but that meant I had to rush through the rest of my morning routine. No regrets. That extra hot shower was the jolt I needed this morning.

I pulled on my favorite gray slacks, a mustard colored-floral print blouse, and navy-blue flats. No time to dry my hair, so I twisted my hair into an office appropriate bun, not the messy one I would have done if I was staying home. Grabbed my to go coffee and then headed for the door.

"Bye, Archie." He flicked his tail from his perch by the front window.

I blasted classic rock, singing badly at the top of my lungs. As the guitar riffs and drums blasted over the airwaves, it cleared the cobwebs. When I slide into the office parking lot, I was ready to conquer the day.

Chapter Ten: Heather

I started pulling things out of my closet, taking them down the hall to our guest room. This used to be Tyler's room. Though there was no trace of him here now.

Gone were the dump trucks, action figures, dinosaurs, and building blocks. Later, those were later replaced with game controllers, soccer cleats, and car magazines. Now it was my blue and yellow guest room.

I laid out my clothing on the bed so I could look at it. We were going to be there for eight days. Well, ten but the first and last day were travel days, so full days for doing vacation stuff were eight days.

We had originally said a week, but extended it slightly after we started talking out the plans. It sounded like we all needed a break. For me, it wasn't so much a break as it was a distraction until I could figure out what to do in this new chapter of life.

I looked at the piles of leggings and tunics, jeans and blouses, skirts or dresses.

"Decisions, decisions." I stepped back to look at my clothing.

At least, the planning and the packing were giving me something to focus on each day instead of wandering around in this massive house like a ghost of myself. What did I used to do with my time?

With the trip, I had menus planned and was researching restaurants, must sees. And with the trip in just less than two weeks, I was focused on packing, just in case I wanted to go shopping for new things before.

I looked at the piles of clothing.

No, I probably wouldn't need to go shopping.

Also, I'd received the treasure hunting book that started all of this. It had arrived a few days after Amy proposed the trip, and I'd been binge reading it since. I was hooked. This was going to be fun.

Also, since we were a registered team, I had been perusing the online forums. It was fun to see what all the other teams were doing. There were only a dozen that were trying for this Fort Aston one. Most were going for the two on the West Coast. One was in San Diego and the other in Seattle.

It didn't sound like any other team was actively searching for the Fort Aston one, just that those were the ones that had registered for it. I hoped that meant we wouldn't have any competition, giving us a better chance to find it, at least I hoped.

I picked up a few blouses, moving them around, trying out this cream top with that black skirt. The red one with... maybe with the black skirt instead.

No, maybe with these navy shorts? I thought, holding them up.

"Whatcha got going on here?" Jason said, coming into the guest room.

"I'm trying to figure out what to pack. It's a long trip."

"Is it this long?" He waved his hand over the piles of clothes.

"Well, yeah. We will be doing treasure hunting, so I need yoga pants, tennis shoes. Then, if we go out to dinner or to a bar, I want something nicer, like this." I held up a sundress.

"I have always loved you in this one." He stepped closer, wrapping his arms around my waist, pulling me to him, then kissing my neck.

I giggled as I let the sundress drop onto the bed. Turning into him, I wrapped my arms around his neck as he kissed me further.

"You know I love having the house to ourselves now." His voice soft in my ear. He took my hand and led me to our bedroom.

Forty-five minutes later, I was back to looking at my clothes after the pleasant distraction. I loved when he was home. It made the house feel less empty and lonely.

Plus, we could have spontaneous moments like that which were definitely a perk of not having the boys home any longer. No more rushed moments. No more hiding and hoping they didn't knock on our door. We could take our time and have those fun liaisons.

This was the third or fourth time in just the last few weeks. My face warmed as I remembered.

Settling on my wardrobe, I folded each item and then left it in the guest room. It would be out of the way until I needed it in a little less than two weeks. I silently clapped my hands.

Exciting! I clapped, looking once more before going to join Jason in the living room.

"Wanna go to dinner?" Jason asked.

"Oh, um, yes. That sounds fun." I had nothing else planned for dinner, thinking we could do something simple like sandwiches and maybe I could heat the soup I had frozen.

"Great."

We got our shoes on and hopped in the car. This was another thing I loved about being an empty-nester. The ability to just jump in the car and go to any restaurant without worrying about if the boys would eat it, would they behave, and would we have to wait for a table? A table for two was always easier.

"Want to go to Clarke's Steakhouse?"

"Oh, that sounds good. We haven't been there in a while."

"Perfect."

He steered the car towards the restaurant roughly 10 miles away. It gave us time to reconnect and chat as we drove over. I was still very much in love with my husband. I definitely picked the right man. We'd been together since we were fourteen years old and had known each other since elementary school.

Remembering the years together, I smiled, reaching for his free hand.

"I'm a lucky woman."

"I feel like the lucky one." He smiled, squeezing my hand.

We arrived at Clarke's a few minutes later to find that the parking lot was only half full.

"I guess we beat the dinner rush."

"Good timing." He said, as we got parked.

"Or the fact we eat so early."

"Or that."

We laughed. The hostess greeted us when we stepped inside. The restaurant was a time warp back to the 1960s with the dark wood, dim lighting and jewel toned decor. We were seated quickly. The server told us the specials and took our drink order.

"Do we want an appetizer?" I asked as I skimmed the menu.

"Stuffed mushrooms?"

"Sounds good to me."

Neither of the boys would have eaten mushrooms, especially these. They were stuffed with shrimp. They would have wanted mozzarella sticks or the loaded french fries. It was nice to have something different.

"I'm thinking of getting the porterhouse. You?"

"The six ounce New York strip."

"Good choice." He smiled at me, causing my stomach to flutter. He still had me blushing like a schoolgirl. I loved him.

The server came back with our drinks, dropped off a loaf of in-house made bread, and then took our order. As she left, I cut a piece of bread.

"So, are you excited about your trip?" Jason asked.

"I am. It sounds so fun."

"I'm happy for you. You've been so... I don't know the right word, but almost depressed."

"Yeah, I guess."

It was true. I'd been moping around trying to find my purpose in life now that my boys had grown up without my permission, I might add. I'd looked for a job, applying to a few things, but nothing has panned out yet. I would get more serious about it after the trip.

All my life I wanted to be a mom; knew I was built to be a mom. I just hadn't realized that my boys would grow up and not need me. Actually, I knew that, but it happened faster than I thought it would and before I was ready.

There are all the baby books on what to expect and websites giving information on the stages, development, and all of that, but I was not prepared for the letting go part of parenting. In each new phase, from sleepovers to sports camps, I learned a new level of independence for them and a slight mourning period for me.

"I can't believe Amy thinks you all can find a treasure." He chuckled softly as he buttered a piece of bread.

I laughed, mildly offended, "and you don't?"

"You're all smart enough, but nobody has even found one treasure yet."

"Yeah, but at least we have a few clues already, so that helps. Plus, I'll have Amy and Marissa there. They are probably the smartest people I know in my life."

"You and Denise are pretty smart, too."

"Yeah, we are."

But Amy had been the valedictorian for our high school class. Then again, when she graduated from college. She had always tutored me throughout school. Had it not been for her, I wouldn't have even graduated.

Marissa was the CEO of a company for a software program that she created. She built it to an enormously success company all while raising four children. If that wasn't smart, I didn't know what was.

I still wasn't clear on what Denise did, but something at a women's shelter. I didn't understand what her role was there. I know that the organization used Marissa's software though, because sometimes they would talk shop.

"But you know you are just as smart as your friends, don't you?" His eyes stared through me. His faith in me had me falling in love with him.

"I guess."

At that moment, our server came up with our salads and drink refills.

"Steaks should be out soon." The server smiled.

Jason dug into his salad. All talk of my trip and if I was or wasn't smart ended. Thank goodness because after my job search, I didn't feel bright. I felt useless.

Our entrées arrived, which quelled conversations further, except for the polite exchange about our food being good. My steak and broccoli were cooked to perfection. It was heaven on a plate, but was more food than I could eat at once.

"Are you getting dessert?" He asked as he ate the last bite of his food.

"Seriously? I'm thinking of getting a doggy bag."

"Oh." His disappointment was clear.

"But don't let that stop you. I know you like the cheesecake."

"Um, maybe."

The server showed up at that moment, "Are y'all thinking dessert?"

"He is. I'm full. Can I get a box?"

"Yes, of course. What can I get for you?"

Jason ordered the chocolate cheesecake to-go.

"Wanna catch a movie?" He asked.

"We have food to get in the fridge."

"Right. We can find something at home."

With that, we headed home for a quiet middle-aged married night at home.

Chapter Eleven: Marissa

The trip was now a week out. I was convinced that everything was going to fall apart with me gone. The ladies and I have been planning this for a few weeks now, but my family seemed to forget it was coming.

I was depending on Mike to step right into my shoes, but that was probably expecting too much from him. He was a good man, a great husband, and a patient, wonderful father, but he hadn't had to do much around the house because I did it all. He also worked extremely hard and didn't always separate work and home.

My thoughts were interpreted by Olivia hollering for me from upstairs.

"Mom? Mooom!"

I mumbled just loud enough to be audible, which always forced her to come to me, instead of bellowing at me like I was an unpaid housemaid or something.

"Mom, did you hear me?" She said from the stairs.

"Yes, yes, I did. The Wilsons down the road heard you."

"Whatever." She rolled her eyes. "Don't forget, I need you to take me shopping for Audrey's party and I have that volleyball tournament. You have to take me, Audrey, and Hannah. Plus, it's my turn to bring the water and snacks for everyone."

"What? When?"

"Next week. The tournament is in Cypress. It's all day there. Then, for shopping, I thought about the Galleria. Then you'll need to drop us all at Audrey's house."

"I won't be in town, Liv."

"What? I told you last week."

"And I told you three weeks ago that I'll be out of town."

"What am I supposed to do? I need you to drive us."

"You'll need to figure it out. Maybe one of the other parents can take you. You also have a few friends that drive, or ask your dad."

I turned my attention back to my computer. I was working on a list for my assistant Elliot to handle while I was gone. Looking ahead to what we had planned for the company, this was the only time I could get away.

"Mom, seriously, I need you."

"Well, I need a break, so I'm going and you'll have to figure this out."

"You're the worst." She stomped off.

I wanted to throw a whatever or two her way, but I let it roll and got back to my instructions for Elliot. After those were done, I started on the ones for my family. Mom and dad's medication schedule was the most important thing, followed by the girls' activities.

I had ordered meals to be delivered each day from a local caterer. I have used them before when I was working a lot. They are excellent and it would be one less thing I had to worry about.

I wasn't as worried about Mike or the kids. They would be fine. It was my folks that I was most worried about. They didn't always eat if I wasn't there to ensure they did, and I couldn't depend on Mike or the kids to remember to feed them. Mom rarely thought of it and dad never really had to cook, as mom used to handle it all until a few years ago when she became ill.

The final straw had been when she nearly burned down their house. She forgot she was cooking and went outside to work in her garden. She only remembered when the fire alarms went off and the first flicks of fire were visible from the yard.

Getting the call about the fire had been the scariest day. I knew mom had been getting forgetful and distracted, but I hadn't realized how bad it had gotten. That's when the decision was that they needed to live with us.

"Whatcha doin'?" Ella came in, plopping down on the couch.

"Working on instructions for when I'm gone next week."

"Oh, that's what has Olivia all upset up there."

"Yeah, I'm just a taxi for that girl." I mumbled, but then looked up at my youngest and smiled. "You'll be fine without me. The only one I'm not worried about."

"I learned from the best." She rolled onto her back and pulled out her phone.

We sat there quietly while I finished. I saved just as my dad came in.

"Am I supposed to take a pill now?"

"Not yet, dad. With dinner."

"Oh, that's right." He sat with a dazed, almost blank, look on his face.

"You, okay?"

"Uh? Oh, yeah. Just a little headache."

I looked at him for a moment. He didn't seem like himself. Last time this happened, his blood pressure was too high. I stood and went into the kitchen, bringing back the blood pressure cuff.

"Here, let's just check your blood pressure." Pushing his sleeve up slightly, I then attached the cuff. "Okay, relax. Feet flat."

I pushed the button, and then we waited. The machine buzzed as it filled up. I smiled at him. He returned the gesture.

Okay, good, he wasn't having a stroke, at least at this moment. I thought.

The machine stopped, and the display read 170 over eighty. Too high.

"Alright, why don't we take you over to the hospital? Do you need to use the restroom?"

"Hm? Oh, no. I'm okay."

I got his shoes, gave Ella some instructions to watch her grandmother, and then I drove my dad to the hospital. I tried to keep him talking by chatting and asking him questions.

"When did you get the headache?"

"This morning, I think."

"Are you sleeping, okay?"

"I suppose." He mumbled.

"What about other things? Anything else seem off or not right."

"I don't know. Maybe I'm peeing more."

"Does it burn or hurt?" *Could this be a urinary tract infection?*

"Not really." He paused. "Maybe a bit, but mostly just going a lot."

"I think you could have a urinary tract infection."

I pulled into the parking lot and ran around to help my dad out. We made our way through the lot to the urgent care clinic.

"Hi, please sign in, then have a seat. We'll call you back up in a moment."

I filled in his name and reason, then we had a seat. He seemed okay, but I was worried. As I watched him from the corner of my eyes, he put his hand to his head and seemed to sway.

"Dad?"

"I'm okay. Maybe I should have taken something for this headache."

"I thought about that, but without knowing what's wrong, I didn't know what to give you. Let's see what they say."

"Mr. Walker?"

"Here." I said, as I helped dad to his feet.

The nurse took us back to the exam room, then took dad's vitals. His blood pressure was still high.

I gave her the list of his meds.

"And he takes the blood pressure medicine daily?"

"Yes. I ensure he takes them all as directed. I have a tracker."

"Okay, good."

"Mr. Walker, are you having any urinary issues? Pain, frequency?"

"Frequency, maybe a bit of pain."

"Well, let's get a sample. Restroom is down the hall, cups are in there. Just write your name, then you can just leave the sample on the counter. I'll go get it when you're done."

I walked with dad down the hall.

Picking up a cup, I handed it to him. "Here are the cups. Just make sure you put your name on it like she said. I'll be right in the hallway if you need me."

He simply smiled, grabbed a cup, and started writing his name on it. I closed the door as I stepped out, smiling at another nurse who walked by. I checked the time.

Damn, I needed to get home.

I sent a text off to Mike asking if he could handle dinner, or at least order something for us. He replied within seconds that he would.

The door opened and dad stepped up holding his pee.

"Dad, put it on the counter there." I pointed to the spot in the bathroom. "Now wash your hands."

"I'm not a child." He laughed, but I could tell he still wasn't himself.

I worried I wouldn't be able to go on this trip now. *Dang it*. But if it meant being there for my sweet father, it was worth giving up.

The nurse came to get his sample, and we headed back to the exam room to wait. It was going to take a while before they would have to results. I didn't know if a doctor would come check on us or if they would wait until the results came in.

Dad laid back on the exam table while I checked my emails, answered a few. Work never stopped.

Then I got a text from Olivia asking if I could take her over to her friend's house. When I told her I couldn't, I got a lot of attitude through the airwaves.

For the love of... I thought. This kid was going to be the death of me.

Thirty minutes later, the doctor came in.

"How are you feeling, Mr. Walker?"

"My head hurts, and I need to pee again."

"We can get you to the restroom in a moment. The headache is likely from the high blood pressure, but you also have a UTI. It doesn't look bad enough for a hospital stay, yet. We'll get you on some antibiotics and you should be good as new."

"And his confusion?" I asked.

"It should go away after he gets going on the meds." He started doing a check-up. "You feel good otherwise?"

"Yes, feeling pretty good usually."

The doctor did a quick physical exam. The usual listening to his heart, looking in his throat, and asking him to breathe deeply a few times.

"Well, lungs sound good. Everything else checks out. I'll get you those prescriptions sent over to your pharmacy and we'll get you out of here."

"What about for his headache? Can he just take any over-the-counter pain reliever?"

"Yes. None should interfere with his current or the new medicines. I increased his blood pressure dosage slightly, which will help. The after care summary notes to follow up with his regular doctor on the dosage."

"Great. Thank you."

Minutes later, we were back in the car and on the way to the pharmacy. I gave him something for his headache, so I hoped it helped him.

Waiting in the car, I got a text from Mike.

Son of a... He got stuck at work and couldn't pick up dinner.

"Mike couldn't get dinner, so we'll have to stop on the way home."

"Can we stop at Larry's?"

"You think you should eat barbecue with your blood pressure?"

"The doc didn't say I couldn't. I should be good to go once I get the drug in me."

I thought about it. Since I didn't have a better idea, I guess we would do it, but I'd monitor his blood pressure.

"Fine, but you're only getting the chicken or turkey. No beef."

He moaned, but agreed.

We got to the front of the drive-thru pick up line at the pharmacy.

"It's not ready yet. Want to circle around?" The technician asked.

No, but I agreed, and we pulled out of line, driving around to wait. While we waited, I put in a pickup order at Larry's. Then sent the kids a message saying we were picking up dinner and currently waiting at the pharmacy.

I threw my phone in my lap, putting my head back on the seat. Dad was snoozing a bit, so why not get a few Zs myself? I was almost in the zone when my phone chimed.

Finally.

But it was Jackson asking when I'd be home with dinner. I'd sent him a text, so why was he asking? I knew the answer. He was impatient.

Me: Soon.

Jackson: I don't have much time between studying.

Me: Jack, I'm trying.

Jackson: Fine. I'll just starve.

Me: Fix a sandwich if you are that hungry, or wait, and I'll be there soon.

Jackson: K

He might not have Olivia's attitude, but he could be needy and lazy. I just hope he really was putting this much energy into studying as he seemed to be.

It was another twenty minutes before I received the text message saying it was ready. I had to drive back around and get in line again. Another ten minutes in line before we finally had the new medicines in hand.

Then I made my way over to Larry's BBQ to pick up our order.

Dad looked over and smiled.

"You feeling better?" I asked.

"Yeah, head isn't pounding as much."

"Glad to hear it. Once we get home, we'll get you fixed up with the other meds. Okay?"

"Thanks. You do a lot for me and your mother. I don't take that for granted."

"Aw, thanks, dad. I'm happy I can do this for you both. You've both set a good example for me growing up."

I squeezed his hand.

The line at Larry's wasn't too bad, but it was slow. I could kick myself for not just running in to grab my order, but I wanted to stay near dad, just in case. Once it was our turn, it was quick.

All the way home, all I could think was about the trip. I needed a break more than anything, but how could I leave when these people couldn't even figure out dinner for one night without me?

Mike wanted to help, but he was busy at work. Heck, even when he was home, he was either still in work mode or he was playing video games. I enabled it.

The kids didn't help, only Jackson drove, but with his classes and studies, he never helped. Olivia had no interest in driving and wanted everyone to do things for her. Ella was willing to help, but was still a bit too young to get her license. Maybe next year she would want to learn.

I sighed.

"You good, Mar?" Dad asked.

"Just... a lot going on."

"Well, you'll have fun with your girlfriends next week."

I looked at him as a lump formed in my throat.

"I can't go, dad. Y'all need me."

He reached over, taking my hand.

"Daughter, we'll be fine. You need this for you."

I studied my sweet, wonderful father. He couldn't drive any longer, so I couldn't count on him for that, but I know, as long as he felt well, he would handle things around the house for me.

"Okay, I'll still go."

Chapter Twelve: Denise

I fluffed my hair, trying to add some volume. Laughing at myself when it flattened out.

"Well, I guess this is as good as it gets."

I was meeting Sidney and Max for dinner. She'd graduate in about six weeks. Hopefully, I was well enough to watch her walk across the stage. Thankfully, my surgery was scheduled for the following week, so at least the timing of that worked out.

This girl's trip with my friends was going to be a test for my health. What could I endure? Would they be able to tell?

My symptoms were mostly under control now that the doctor had me on medicines to help lessen the bloating and diarrhea. It was mostly fatigue that I had still had to deal with.

Grabbing my purse, keys, and cell phone, I headed to the car. I cranked up the air condition and the radio as I headed towards the restaurant.

I thought about the upcoming trip. Just a few more days and I'd be on a plane heading to meet my friends in Florida. I didn't know if we could solve the mystery and find the treasure, but for me, that wasn't what this was about. For me, this was to make fun memories with my girlfriends before cancer treatments. The morbid part of me thought this could be my last trip ever.

"No, I was going to fight."

I had a lot to live for and her name was Sidney. Her beautiful smile and sweet voice. She was loving and generous.

She would be a wonderful mother someday, and I had every intention of being there to see the baby. Even though I wasn't a fan of marriage, I thought Max was the perfect partner for my daughter. They were the sweetest couple and would make excellent parents someday.

I pulled into the parking of Trucker's Bar and Grill. I scanned the parking lot for their maroon Camry. I spotted it three down from the door. There wasn't an empty space near them, so I drove around to the next row.

"Mom!" Sid's voice came from near the door.

"Hey." I waved as I headed towards her.

"Max has a table saved. I ordered you an iced tea."

"Perfect."

We made our way through the crowd to a table where my handsome son-in-law was waiting for us.

"Hi, mom." He stood to hug me.

"Hi, sweetie. You look good." I smiled.

I picked up the menu. "What's good here?"

"The fish and chips are good." Max said.

"I like the Trucker burger." Sid said.

"Is that what you guys are getting then?" I was trying to eat better, so I was looking at the salads, but the burger sounded good.

The waiter brought over our drinks. "Y'all ready to order?"

We each placed our order. I ended up getting the Trucker burger with cheese and curly fries.

"Alright. I'll get your order in. It'll be out soon." He left us.

"Are you excited about your trip?" Sid asked.

"Oh, it doesn't seem like it's real yet. I guess when I start packing, or maybe when I get to the airport, it will feel real."

"It's so interesting that you're going on a treasure hunt." Max smiled.

"Yeah, it's … interesting." I had mixed feelings about the actual treasure hunting part, but Amy and Heather were both excited about it, so I was trying to be enthusiastic about it.

"Do you think y'all can find the treasure?"

"I honestly don't know, but it will be fun to just get away for a few days."

"Your trip is a week-long, right?" Sidney asked.

"A little over a week, but yes."

"I'm happy for you, mom. This will be so much fun for you."

"Thanks." I smiled. "But enough about me. Tell me about what you all have going on. Good end to the semester? How is the house coming together?"

"I'm so glad that my classes are nearly over, and I can finally move on."

"I'll be glad when you have more free time." Max teased.

"I know. Me too." She laughed. "I miss trashy tv shows and fun romance novels."

"Any job offers yet?"

"Not yet, but I had another interview with that medical equipment company. The one I was telling you about. It sounds like a wonderful company and challenging work."

"Oh, that one sounded like a good fit. Good luck."

Our food arrived. The burger was huge.

"Wow, this is big." I smiled as I cut it in half. The juice of it running out. It was piled high with fresh tomato slices, sweet onions, and crispy lettuce. I took a bite and nearly passed out from the pure joy of that bite. I'd been eating mostly bland food lately. Less salt and fat, almost no sugar. It was an adjustment, but I had felt better and had lost a few pounds. This was my first cheat in nearly a month.

"I told you the burger was good." Sidney said before taking a bite of her own burger.

I simply nodded as I took another big bite, then followed that with a salty curly fry dipped in their special ketchup. I would surely pay for this poor decision later, but I was going to enjoy each bite.

I ate until I was full, forcing myself to stop. Something I was slowly learning to do.

"That was good."

"It was. This is one of our favorite places."

"I can't believe you haven't been here before." Max said.

"Well, it won't be the last." I silently said a prayer that it wouldn't be my last.

The server dropped off the check. I took it, did a quick skim of the bill before dropping my credit card down.

"Thanks, mom." They both said.

I smiled, "You're welcome."

The server came back with my card and the receipt. I signed it.

"Alrighty, ready?"

"Yep."

We made our way through the crowded restaurant and waded through the line at the door. Finally, out in the parking lot, we stopped at their car.

"Do you have to get home, or do you want to play cards or something at my place?"

"Unfortunately, I need to get home to finish a paper, so we'll have to take a rain check," Sid said, leaning over to hug me. "Love you, mama. Thanks for dinner."

"My pleasure."

Max leaned in for a hug, also thanking me for dinner. "We'll see you again after the trip, yes?"

"Definitely. I'll bring fun souvenirs."

I waved as I walked to my car, then watched as they drove away. My throat tightened. I couldn't die. I would miss these little moments with them. They would miss them with me.

I pulled out of the parking spot, but I really didn't feel like going home. My dad and stepmother were on a cruise, so I couldn't call them. I thought of my friends. Couldn't think of any that would be available for a pop-over. Most still had young children at home and schedules full of sports and scouts, homework and dinner.

I sighed, but then an idea popped into my head.

"Lemon lime snow cone at Hugo's."

Hugo's was an institution here. He had been serving ice cream, snow cone, and treats to the community for over forty years. I worked there a few summers as a teen as did Sidney.

That's where she met Max, actually. They had worked together one summer, and as they say, the rest is history.

I parked in the crushed shell parking lot and got in the long line. I watched the various groups waiting. Families with bouncy children, young couples on dates, and older, long-married couples. I felt a little silly standing here alone, but I wanted a little treat without the guilt, or at least less guilt.

"Oh, hey, Denise." Hugo said when I reached the front. At nearly eighty years old, he still liked to work every day.

"Hi, Mr. Hugo." I smiled at the friendly face behind the counter.

"What can I getcha?"

"Lemon lime snow."

"Good choice." He turned to his grandson, Norris. "Lemon lime for Denise."

"Comin' right up," Norris shouted.

"So, hey, how's the sweet newlyweds doing?"

"Oh, they are wonderful. I just had dinner with them."

"How nice. Give them my love."

"I will. Thanks."

I stepped to the next window and waited for my snow cone. I tried to be calm and casual, even though I felt silly standing there alone with all the families and couples. Smiling at those closest to me.

"Oh, hey, Denise." Came a deep voice nearby.

"Steve, hi." It was my high school boyfriend and longtime crush. I hadn't seen him in a while. "How are you?"

"Good, good. You look good." He smiled.

"Thanks. You too."

He looked around. "You here with someone?"

Why? I thought, but didn't want to say that. Last I heard, he was happily married to Brenda Lucio, the girl he broke up with me for. They had two children, the dog, and a big house on a hill. The all-American family.

"No, just had dinner with my daughter- and son-in-law. Thought a snow cone was a nice treat."

"Nice." He toed the ground with his shoe. "I don't know if you heard, but Brenda and I got a divorce last year."

"Oh, no I hadn't. Sorry to hear."

"Thanks. It was long overdue." He smiled. "So, it's funny I ran into you, huh?"

Crap. No.

"Why's that?"

"Just thinking maybe we could go out sometime. Talk about old times, see what happens." He moved closer.

I stepped back and fought the urge to full body shutter. Instead, I stiffened my back and stood taller.

"Uh, no, that's okay. I'm busy." I said firmly.

"Wha...But...?" He stuttered.

Thankfully, Norris called my name, so I excused myself.

"Watch that one," Norris whispered. "He is a huge player. That's why his wife left him."

"I can only imagine. Thanks, Norris." I took my snow cone and hopped into my car without a backward look.

People often asked me why I enjoyed being single. Example one, Steve Brusier from high school. Creepy didn't even begin to describe that encounter. I didn't fight the shiver as it shook through my body.

"Gross!" I yelled at the windshield and then laughed. Then I bite the lemon lime ice and enjoyed my little treat as I drove home.

When I got home, I threw the snow cone cup in the trash and went to my room to finish packing. My trip was less than twelve hours away. I couldn't wait.

I double checked what I had already put in my hot pink rolling bag. Eight days meant a minimum of eight outfits, plus I threw in two dresses in case we went somewhere nice.

I held up my tankini swimsuit. It covered enough of my sin that I wasn't embarrassed going in public in it. The shorts camouflaged my upper thighs and the fact I hadn't shaved as closely as I once did. The pleating on the top hid the roll of fat and extra pounds around my middle. This would be my first time wearing it.

I zipped up my bag and rolled it to the front door. Eleven hours to go.

I hadn't been on a plane in a few years. I hoped I didn't flub up going through security. It seemed easy enough, but I was an overthinker, so I pulled out my phone to reread the security procedures.

Easy peasy.

The flight for me was only a few hours, but I just hoped my stomach didn't give me too much trouble. As long as my medicine continued to work, I should be okay. Plus, drinking enough water seemed to help as well.

I had always thought that people with colon cancer had no symptoms, but I was one of the lucky ones or unlucky, depending on how you look at it. It was the reason I had a diagnosis so early and my cancer hadn't yet spread much. I shouldn't have put off screening like I did or it might have been caught even sooner.

Thankfully, my doctor had given me the okay to travel and postpone treatment until I return. They couldn't get me in for surgery for two months, anyway. It would be a few weeks after our return from the trip and the week after Sid's graduation.

Leading up to that, it was a lot of lab tests and prepping. My doctor, Doctor Ruiz, had me see a therapist.

"In counseling, you can talk about all your fears and worries. I like to offer that to my patients."

"Thanks." I hadn't yet seen her, but my appointment was set for when I got back from the trip.

"I think it's wonderful that you are taking this trip. It sounds like a lot of fun."

"Yeah." I mumbled. I was still numb. Hoping that I would wake up from this nightmare.

Cancer.

"You don't sound happy about it." She studied me.

"I am. Just worried about the obvious."

"I understand, but I think self-care and the support you'll have with your friendships are just as important to the surgery and chemotherapy. Again, support and these happier moments are things of comfort during treatment. My patients with those things do so much better than those without it."

Looking over at my bag by my front door, I remembered her words. I had no idea what I was going to do about telling my friends, but especially Sidney.

Instead of thinking about it further, I went to the kitchen to take my medicine. They had me on a few things now for pain and discomfort. It helped with the bloating feeling.

Two weeks with my friends, I just hoped I could hide this from them, or at least until I was ready to share my secret.

Doctor Ruiz had encouraged me to confide in those closest to me like family and friends, but I just couldn't bring myself to do it yet. If I got the nerve to do it on this trip, I would, but honestly, I didn't want to put a damper on the vibe. We'll see.

I still thought of all the years with my mother. The mental torture she put me through was fresh in my mind.

She always manipulated the truth and my feelings to keep me under her thumb. It wasn't until I was in college that I realized what she was doing. Immediately, I cut off contact and only came back once she was in hospice. She was hateful, saying she didn't want me there one minute and then the next, begging me not to leave her, then right back to screaming at me.

As she was facing her own mortality, I could understand to a point why she'd be so nasty to me. But if she was anyone else, I would have walked away. I was her only daughter; and thought I should be there for her and was until the end. Sadly, I mostly remember her hateful words to me, nothing much else.

I simply whispered I loved her as she took her last breath, then walked away numb and confused. I know I wasn't my mother, but I didn't want to treat anyone in my life that way.

With my bag packed, I wandered around the house, ensuring it was ready for me to go out of town. Since I didn't have a significant other, children, or pets to mess up the house, there wasn't anything that needed attention.

So, I decided to take a bath. I grabbed my tablet so I could read while I soaked in the tub.

This could be my last bath for a long time, or at least I assumed until after the surgery and treatments. I had every intention of enjoying it.

I lit a candle, started the water running. As it filled, I dropped a bath bomb in. The floral scent filled the room as it released the fragrant smells.

I stripped and then slid into the warm, scented water.

"Ah." I sighed out.

I grabbed my tablet to pull up my current book. It was a fun rom-com by my favorite author. This was nice. An hour later, I was relaxed and ready for bed.

I sent a group text to let them know I was ready to go. I drifted off to sleep with thoughts of white sand beaches and frozen drinks.

Chapter Thirteen: Amy

The blast of my alarm woke me up. My eyes and brain came awake.

Today! The trip is today.

I looked around, realizing that I had actually slept really well last night and in our bedroom, of all places. Not the guest room, like usual.

We hadn't fought last night, at least nothing more than a little harmless bickering over the remote and what television show to watch. It was playful and led to naked time, which we hadn't had in a while. It was *nice* and probably contributed to my good night's sleep.

I stretched and only just realized that Scott wasn't in bed. It was still dark out. Perhaps he was just working in the office. I got up, making my way to the bathroom, and then in search of coffee and then I'd look for my husband. Priorities.

There was a fresh pot of coffee waiting for me, but no Scott. I frowned, then poured a mug full of the hot coffee, adding a splash of flavored creamer, then headed down the hall. First peeking in his office. His laptop was here, so he hadn't gone to work. Maybe he was out for a jog or at the gym.

I just hope he comes home in time to see me off.

Sipping in the coffee, I headed back down the hall. I put a scoop of dried cat food in Archie's bowl, checked his water, and then cleaned his litter box.

Next, I headed for the shower. I lingered only a moment under the hot water before lathering head to toe, rinsing, and hopping out. I'd likely take another once I got to Florida. I always felt like I was covered in germs after traveling all day.

I put on some comfy wide leg gray slacks. They were soft as butter and casual enough for a day of traveling, but nice enough that I didn't feel frumpy. I pulled on a mustard colored short-sleeved blouse and a cardigan as I knew I'd get cool on the airplane. Then I slipped my feet into a pair of black loafers. These would be easy to take on and off through airport security.

I packed a few last-minute things and then dragged my bags down the hall. I probably over packed, but if our scale was to be believed, they were both under the 50 pounds free limit. Plus, I had a large purse, and a backpack stuffed with things.

After one too many delays and cancellations at the airport, I started taking at least one day's worth of stuff on the plane with me. The flight had been a bargain bin price, but that meant two layovers. I had my eReader loaded with a dozen new books and created a new music playlist to listen to. That should get me from Baltimore to Pensacola, Florida. We had a rental car lined up.

Marissa would be the first to land, then Heather, then Denise and I would arrive at almost the same time. I did a goofy little dance as I thought of seeing my friends again after so long. The treasure hunt was a fun bonus to the trip.

I shot off a text to Scott, then called a ride share. Standing in the living room, I peeked out the front window. How long before the car would get here? Looking down, nobody had been assigned yet. *Damn.*

I sighed and stared out at our quiet suburban street. A cat or maybe a raccoon was nosing around in the bushes across from us. I watched the shadow of it for a moment, before it disappeared on the side of my neighbor's house.

A minute later, Scott's truck pulled into the driveway. I watched as he frantically hopped out and came into the house.

"I'm so sorry!"

"I thought you were mad at me or something."

"No, just poor time management at the gym." He hugged me. "Do you need a ride to the airport?

"I just called a car."

"Can you cancel?"

I looked at the app. My request was still not assigned, so said a little curse as I hit cancel.

"Alright. Canceled."

"Great. Let's go!" He hooked his thumbs towards the door.

"Let me just say bye to Archie."

"He's not even going to care." He laughed.

"I will though."

I went to find him. He was sprawled out on the windowsill of the guest bedroom. It was his favorite spot overlooking the backyard. He could bird watch, soak up the sun, and nap all at the same time.

"Bye, Archie."

He flicked his tail and looked up at me. I kissed his ginger head, giving it one last scratch under his chin.

Scott grabbed my bags for me, loading them into his truck.

"Are you sure you brought enough?" He chuckled.

"It's a week-long trip. You just never know." I shrugged.

"One of those things I love about you." He kissed me softly, then we climbed into his truck. He steered us down our quiet street. There were few cars on the roads as we headed towards the airport.

We made small talk. I could tell he was picking topics and his words carefully, so we didn't have a fight before I was gone for a week. I was too excited to fight.

"So, you got that new release out without issues, huh?" He asked.

"Yes, an enormous relief to have it done and stable before this trip."

"I bet. Is Heather still sending y'all lists?"

"Yes, you know Heather." We laughed.

"Oh, yeah, she's a hoot."

As we neared the airport, traffic got a little heavier, but not awful. Checking the clock, still should make it with plenty of time.

"Worried?" He looked over at me.

"Nah, should still get there with time to spare."

"No, I mean, worried about us?"

"What about us?"

"I mean, we're good, right?"

"Absolutely."

We hadn't been fighting as much. I was really trying to not be grumpy. Having the major release done at work had helped my mood. My team was back in operations mode, so it should run smoothly until we had another big release planned.

Though I wouldn't say it out loud, I was also looking forward to this break from him, from us. No point in saying anything to him about that. It would just cause a fight and I wanted to leave on the happy high from our night together and this sweet gesture of driving me to the airport. He really was a good man.

"Okay, good. I love you." He smiled.

"Love you, too."

I smiled and then looked out the window as the airport came into sight. My stomach fluttered as I got both excited and nervous. An airplane flew overhead as it was landing. I watched it as best I could, but I couldn't see the runway from here.

"Do you want me to come in with you?"

"No, you can't get very far. Just drop me by the departures."

He nodded, then followed the long line that snaked around to the departure area. He pulled to the side. We both got out, and he helped me with my bags.

"Okay, this is it." I said, my stomach fluttering with excitement.

"Yep, I guess so. Don't worry about Archie. I'll take good care of him." He leaned forward to hug me, then gave me a goodbye kiss. "I miss you already."

"I'll miss you." But I'm ready for a break.

I turned to head into the airport while he turned to his truck. I looked over my shoulder just as his truck pulled away from the curb.

I pushed my bags over to the bag drop off area and did the check-in steps. I watched them put my bags on the belt. I said a silent prayer that they would wait for me at the end of my journey.

I headed towards the security line and made the slow walk until it was my turn to go through. It took me three bins to layout all my items, but once I was through, I made my way to the convenient store for a bottle of water and a snack.

After that, I found my gate.

This is happening. It's really happening.

I shot off a text to the group.

See you soon!

Now to kill time until I got there. I pulled out my phone, sending a group text to my children. Aiden and Hannah were the only two that replied. Owen was likely already at work and Noah was probably sleeping, so I'd likely hear from them later.

Next, I flipped over to the forums for the treasure hunt. I wanted to see if anyone was on the same hunt as us. Last time I looked, there wasn't anyone. I hoped that was still the case. Checking the newest threads, it looked like nobody else was actively looking. I mentally high-fived myself.

This was going to be fun.

I read through some posts on the clues. It was still stuck at the one leading to the church. Some teams posted pictures from inside of the gorgeous stained-glass windows. I couldn't wait to see them in person.

I read through some of the discussion, but I couldn't help thinking they were looking at the wrong windows. It had to follow the story of the Commodore. They were guessing scenes from the bible or from the Florida themed room.

Wrong. All wrong.

But, of course, not being there yet, I wasn't sure what the right clue was. I just knew those guesses were wrong.

My thoughts were interrupted as they started to board my flight. I lined up and tried not to squeal with excitement. Just a few more hours until I was in Florida with my best friends on our quest for glory.

Chapter Fourteen: Heather

My flight landed. I looked out the window of the plane as we taxied to towards the gate. This was real, and it was happening now. I wanted to clap and sing out, but I simply sat nice and proper, the way my grandmother taught me.

It took several minutes for us to reach the gate, even though this was a fairly small airport, and then it took several more for people to deplane. I sent Marissa a message that I had arrived.

She replied she was waiting in baggage claim.

Me: I'll be there shortly.

Marissa: See ya soon.

I gathered my things, then made my way off the plane. First stop, restroom. I hated the tiny airplane bathrooms, so I rarely use them. Next, I grabbed a fresh bottle of water.

With that done, I practically sprinted to meet Marissa. I saw her before she saw me.

"Marissa!"

"Hey, girl!"

We hugged.

"You look so great." She said, as our hug ended.

"So do you. I swear you age backwards."

"Ha, you're sweet. A liar, but sweet."

"So, any word from Amy or Denise? Flights on time?"

"No word yet, other than the 'they were on their way' text that they both sent, that we all sent really." She gestured to me. I nodded as I'd been on those. "But, I just checked. Their flights are still showing on time."

"So, we wait for the next hour."

"Yep, but that gives us time to chat."

"Great. Let me grab my luggage and I'll be right back."

I walked over to the carousel that had just come to life with my flight number flashing above it. I watched as bag after bag began dropping, then I recognized my red duffel and a few bags later, my red rolling bag. I lifted them as they got to me, then went back to Marissa.

"You brought two bags too?" She laughed.

"Yeah, I tried to fit it in one, but couldn't."

We sat back for our wait. It was so nice to be here with her. My friend for over twenty years.

"How are your boys?" She asked.

"Busy. Too busy for mom." I laughed.

"Lucky. My kids are so dang needy. I can't believe I was able to get away."

"How are your parents doing?"

"Oh, good days and bad days with mom. Dad is doing well."

We continued to make small talk as we waited for our friends. After nearly an hour, we both got a message from Denise.

Denise: I've landed. Where can I find you beauties?

Marissa: Baggage claim!

Denise: K. On my way

Marissa: See you soon

Before she made it to us, we got another text. This time, it was Amy.

Amy: Queen bitch has arrived!

I cringed, but Marissa laughed as she typed out her reply. Yes, I've been called a prude a few times or a couple hundred times.

Marissa: Get your ass down here to baggage claim!

Amy: Yes, ma'am!

With that, our group would finally be together again.

"Ladies!" We heard a voice call out.

We stood as Denise rushed towards us, catching us both in a hug.

"Oh, it's so good to see you both. It's been too long."

"It really has," Marissa said, giving her another hug.

"I'm so glad we could do this." I said.

"So, Amy just got in too." Denise said, looking over her shoulder.

No Amy yet.

"I'll go wait for my bags and meet you back over here?"

We waited as she went for her luggage and for Amy to join us. Denise joined us before Amy did.

"Amy's not here yet?" Denise said as she brought of her one bag.

"Not yet."

"Is that all you brought?" Marissa pointed at the rolling bag.

"Um, yeah? I'm a simple girl. You know that."

"Are you saying I'm high maintenance?" Marissa laughed.

"Yes, yes, I am," Denise teased.

"Well, you would be right."

"I missed you, ladies." I said.

"I missed you all, too." Denise said.

"Me too."

We stood there a moment, looking around.

"Should we call her?" I asked.

"Maybe."

"I'm here. I'm here." Amy's voice came from behind us. "Sorry, a little kid lost his cookies, if you know what I mean, just as we got to the gate. It was all over the aisle, so they had us wait. The smell, y'all, the smell. People started getting sick all over the place, so they ended up having to get us all out of there. It was awful. I should have texted that we were running late, but it was all I could do to hold it together."

"Girl!" Marissa said as she wrapped her arms around her. "Well, we are so glad you're here."

"Let me grab my bags, then we can hit the road." She turned to the carousel that had her flight number. It was several minutes before bags dropped from the back.

The rest of us stood back, surrounded by our own luggage, and trying to stay out of the way. Denise and Marissa chatted while I people watched.

The dynamics around the luggage carousel were fascinating. There was the jockeying for the best position people. The stand back, acting bored people. The couple barely holding it together as they bickered quietly. The family with kids trying to climb on the luggage.

Amy looked over her shoulder with a smile at us, then grabbed her first bag and then, shortly after, her second. She stacked them and then rolled over to us.

"Alright, bitches, let's get this party started."

We followed the signs to the rental cars. Got checked in, grabbed the keys, and then followed the signs to the parking lot.

"Um, oh, this way." Denise pointed.

Marissa clicked the button, and we followed the sound to a dark blue Chevy Traverse. Marissa pushed the button to open the bag.

"Nice. Should have plenty of room for our bags."

We started loading up our bags, then Marissa in the driver's seat. Denise riding next to her with Amy and me jumping into the second-row bucket seats.

"Wow, this is nice." I said, looking around.

"This is nice." Denise said.

"Okay, ladies, should we grab some dinner before heading out to Fort Aston?"

"I'm starving."

"Me too."

"Yes, let's eat."

We all pulled out our phones to find a place on our route out of Pensacola.

"How about this seafood place?"

"Looks good to me."

"Yep."

"Alright, this party is rolling now."

A few hours later, full and tired, we pulled up to the rental house. It was dark, so I couldn't get a good look at the house, but from what I could tell, it looked just like the pictures.

Stucco walls with stones around windows and lining the corners. I couldn't quite make out the colors, but remembering the pictures, the stucco was beige, and the stones were dark browns. The contrast of colors had caught my eye and drew me to this house. Not to mention the deck overlooking the pool and the beach.

Though this house wasn't right on the beach, it had an unobstructed view and was only a minute or two walk across the street to it. The private pool was an amazing bonus.

"We're here!" I cheered, though quietly, as Denise had dozed off on the drive.

As the car came to a stop, she yawned and stretched.

"Oh, we're here." She mumbled. "Yay."

We hopped out and grabbed bags. Amy got out the code for the keyless entry. As the frosted glass door swung open, we stepped into the large living room, fumbling for a light.

"This is gorgeous." Marissa said, as the lights flooded the living area.

In front of us was the spacious living room with a large denim colored fabric sectional and two matching oversized side chairs. Both had yellow and gray throw pillows. There was a large television mounted on one wall, various beach themed knick-knacks and side tables. Then, across the room from the TV, was an all-glass bar.

"Tomorrow I am heading to the liquor store to stock that." Amy announced.

"I'm exhausted." Denise said. "Let's figure out rooms and then worry about the rest tomorrow."

"Good idea." Marissa said.

We headed down a hallway to find the bedrooms. There were four, which is another reason we picked this one, plenty of space, and we didn't have to double up. The first room was the largest, with a private bathroom.

"Who gets the big one?" I asked as we peeked into the primary bedroom.

"I vote for Amy to get it. This was her idea." Denise said, looking into the room across the hall. "I like this one."

"Yeah, Amy, you take this one. Denise this one, and Marissa and I will pick from the other two." I said.

"I don't want to take it if someone else wants it."

"I just want to sleep." Denise said.

She went into the bedroom across the hall, haphazardly dropping her bag, then sprawled out on the bed. I smiled at her from the hallway.

"Um, I'll take this one at the end of the hall, if that's okay, Marissa?"

I hadn't even seen it yet, but from the listing, they were all more or less the same, except the primary one, which was bigger and included a private bathroom.

"Okay, I'll take this one then, but I will share the bathroom." Amy said.

"Deal." Marissa and I said together.

With that, we all went to our rooms to unwind and go to sleep. I went to the one at the end of the hall, flipping on the light. Inside the room was a lush queen-sized bed with a yellow and blue duvet and four fluffy pillows with the same yellow and blue striped pattern.

Over the bed was a beach themed print of the sand and the surf with seashells dotting the shore. I smiled as I looked around the room. The entire house had a cozy beach theme that was comforting.

"I love it." I mumbled as I fell on to the bed.

This definitely beat moping around my house and feeling useless and alone, wishing I could go back in time to when my boys were toddlers and needed me.

I changed into my pajamas, then went in search of the guest bathroom. Denise was just exiting it.

"Good night." I said.

"Night, see you in the morning." She smiled.

I went through my nightly routine as I took in the simply decorated bathroom in that same beach theme as the rest of the house. The blue, yellow, and gray color scheme was soothing. As I brushed my teeth, I smiled at the cute little fish prints staring at me from their frames on the wall.

After I was done in the bathroom, I made my way to the kitchen to get a glass of water.

"Oh, hey, water too?" Amy asked.

"Yeah, gotta take my old lady pills." I chuckled.

She held up a handful of pills. "Me too, girl. When did we get like this?"

"I have no idea." I filled up my water glass. "Weren't we just running around in pigtails through the sprinkler?"

She chuckled at the memory. "Yeah."

She finished taking her pills, then walked to the window.

"I wish I could see out better." She sighed. "I guess it will wait for morning."

"Yeah, the online pictures looked gorgeous."

"They did."

We said good night, and both headed to our rooms. I tossed and turned a bit in the unfamiliar room, but soon drifted off into a peaceful slumber.

It was still dark when I woke hours later. Checking the clock showed I was up just before six. Of course, but at least I'd get to see the sunrise.

"First official day on vacation." I giggled softly.

I couldn't wait to get started with our treasure hunt. Popping out of bed, I made my way to the bathroom. With a house full of women, I expected it to be occupied, but maybe they were still asleep. It was quite early, and we had gotten in so late. I didn't know their sleep schedules, but I was an early riser.

Something I had done when the boys were young so I could get breakfast made or school lunches packed and clothes laid out for the day. Then, as they got older, I drove them to school early for football practice or track.

With that done, I went to the kitchen. We hadn't been to the store yet, but the host had coffee available, so I headed straight for the pot to start some brewing.

"Oh, already done."

I peeked around. Nobody in sight, but then I saw the sliding door leading to the back deck was cracked a bit and I could see the silhouette of Denise. Finding a coffee mug, I helped myself, then stepped out into the humid, salty air.

"Good morning."

"Oh, good morning. I didn't wake you, did I?" Denise asked.

"Not at all. I'm an early riser. Habit I got into with the boys, that I never broke after they left."

"I understand that." She stared straight ahead.

"Is that why you're up early?" I pointed to the sunrise.

She sighed, "Yeah, just habit. Plus, I wanted to catch the sunrise by the beach."

We both stared out at the water. It was still a bit early, and the sun was just at the edge of the horizon. The sky was still dark with various shades of pink creeping up.

A noise behind us, caused us to jump and turn.

"Sorry, ladies." Marissa said, stepping out. She came and sat next to me. "Ah, just what I've been looking forward to. Coffee on the deck watching the sunrise."

"Did I miss it?" Amy said, coming out behind her.

"Just starting." I said, taking another sip of coffee.

We watched quietly as the sun rose and the beach came into full view. The seagulls flying and squawking to each other. There were sandpipers on the sand. They were just tiny dots from our view, but it was easy to tell what they were.

"Anyone need more coffee?" I asked, breaking the silence.

Both Denise and Amy said they'd like some. I grabbed their mugs.

"I do, too." Marissa said, standing. "I'll come help you."

"Thanks."

We went to the kitchen. I cleaned out the pot and started fresh.

"So, I was thinking today we'd go to the store and then once we have the groceries unloaded, we could head over to the church."

"Well, I was thinking of hitting the liquor store and laying by the pool or on the beach." Marissa chuckled.

"But we came for the treasure."

"I came to spend time with my friends and get a break from my life."

I was stumped at a reply to that.

"I guess… that's why I'm here, too." I stumbled. "But we do need to get groceries and, of course, alcohol."

We laughed together.

The coffee pot beeped, so I started filling mugs. Together, we carried the mugs back to our other friends.

"Do we make a grocery list or wing it?" I asked.

My friends exchanged smirks.

"What? Should I be offended?"

"No, we love you, being you." Amy said.

"What will make you happy?" Marissa asked, leaning over to hug me.

I thought for a moment. I couldn't help that I was a planner. It was just how I was built. "I can make a short list for us, but then we can just grab whatever, I guess."

"Does it hurt?" Amy teased.

"A little bit, yeah." I laughed at myself. "Y'all know I can't help myself."

"We know!" They all said through their laughter at me. It felt good to be with them and not alone. I needed to let go a bit of the planner in me and just enjoy the journey.

Chapter Fifteen: Marissa

Heather had made us a thorough list, so once we were all showered and dressed for the day, we went in search of supplies. First to find a liquor store, followed by groceries.

"Did anyone notice if there was a blender in the house?" Amy asked as we pulled into a spot in front of the Fort Aston's Ales and Spirits store.

"I think I saw one." Heather said.

"Worse case, we have them on the rocks." I suggested. "I don't need a frozen margarita to get drunk."

We laughed as we got out of the car. The chime above the door greeted us as we stepped into the store.

"Hi, y'all. Welcome. Let me know if you need help finding anything." The lady behind the counter greeted.

She was at least twenty years older, with skin that looked like she'd spent too many days in the sun. Dressed in a too-tight top without a bra had me both mortified and cheering for her at the same time. It was a little more of the local scenery than I wanted to see, but if she was confident, more power to her.

We made our way to the tequila, grabbing two bottles and a margarita mix. Next, we picked up a few bottles of wine for dinners and then I grabbed a case of beer. Just some cheap stuff for beach days.

We headed to the checkout. The lady, Flora, as her name badge read, greeted us again.

"Y'all having a party or a really good day at the beach?" She laughed as she rang up each item.

"On vacation. This is for... well, a few days anyway." Amy chuckled.

"Yeah, we'll probably be back." I added.

"Well, we're happy to have you, ladies."

"Do you know of any good lunch spots?" Heather asked. "Seafood or really anything?"

"Oh, sure, we have lots, but you can't go wrong with the Purple Pelican. It's over on Shore Drive. You can't miss it. The entire building is purple. Lindy is the owner. She loves purple." Flora laughed. "It fills up, so I'd go early or call ahead. Get the redfish. It's the best."

"Thanks for the tip." Heather grinned.

We finished up the transaction, thanked Flora, assuring her we'd be back and then loaded in the car again. A few miles away, we pulled into the parking lot of the local grocery store.

Heather grabbed a cart. "Do you think we need two?"

"I think one should get us what we need, at least for a few days or so. Plus, we'll go out for meals too." I said.

She nodded, and we began our shopping. We loaded up the cart with both planned and impulse buys. As I watched the cart fill up, I was kicking myself for not getting a second one.

"Sorry, I didn't realize we'd need a second cart." I apologized to Heather.

"It's okay. I didn't realize we would get this much, either." She grinned.

We got everything paid for and loaded in the car. Amy hopped behind the wheel and started us towards the house.

"So, do we want to eat at the house or head back out for lunch?" Heather asked.

"That pelican place sounds good." Denise said as she read us some of the menu items. "It's not too far from the house, either. A few minutes or so away."

"That sounds like a good plan, then. We'll get this stuff dropped off and then head out." Amy added as she guided the car through the traffic.

"Anyone else find it ironic that we just did all this grocery shopping, but we're going out for lunch?" I pointed out.

"Um?"

"Ha, yeah."

"I'm still down for lunch out."

"Yeah, I didn't disagree with going to lunch, just found it funny." I laughed.

It was a perfect beach day and by the looks of the other cars; it appeared many were planning to take advantage of it. As I looked out the car window, I smiled.

There were the happy families with small children bouncing and grinning in the back seat, and cars full of teenagers with their music blaring drove past us. It had me almost missing my family. Almost.

As if on cue, I got a text. It was Olivia complaining about her volleyball tournament. She had to get a ride from a girl on the team that she didn't always get along with. Nobody else had been available.

I ignored the text, which won me several in a row. I put my phone on silent and looked out the window again. My body relaxed as I watched the palm trees and brightly painted homes. It felt good to put distance between and my family for just a short time.

Though a tinge of guilt tried to creep up, but I quieted the voice by telling it that my family wasn't helpless. They were all grown up enough to be without me for a week or even two if I wanted while I took a much needed break.

The truth was that I had been working so hard to prove that I could run a household and a company without missing a beat, but it was wearing on me. Something had to give soon, or I would have a full mental collapse.

It all started when I was working as a Human Resources Generalist. It was a fairly easy job, though busy at times. It had allowed me to have my family. But at some point, the simple process I had created for my company to track and manage personnel morphed into a company of its own. I quit my job to run my own software business.

When the kids were little, I was building this up, spending a lot of time away from home, but I still tried to be there for them. I attended field trips, class plays, sporting events, all of it. It was a lot of sleepless nights as I tried to do it all.

Ten years later, my company had sixty clients. Correction, now sixty-one. We catered to small companies who had only one to two HR personnel. I could probably step away from the day-to-day operations. We didn't need me to keep working and it would be nice to spend the last years with my youngest two girls. Jackson was still home, too, but I didn't see him much. Perhaps if I was home more, I could spend more time with him, too.

Emma didn't live with us any longer, but I didn't feel like I saw her enough, either. She had her own life now, which left little time for spending with us. I gave her grace on that because she was like me in a lot of ways. Hustle and hold it all together until you break. I closed my eyes. I needed to reach out to her more, tell her this wasn't the way to be, and maybe I should slow down myself.

Then I thought of my parents. They likely didn't have many years left, and it would be nice to have more time with them as well. Especially with mom, she had so few good days. I missed who she once was.

I looked at my friends. Would they think less of me if I quit? Amy caught me looking and smiled. I know she couldn't read my thoughts, but it was reassuring. I'd definitely think about giving up my job.

We pulled up at the house. It was a beautiful place. We'd gotten lucky to rent one right on the water. I couldn't wait to get back and layout by the pool with the sound of the gulf in the background.

We unloaded the groceries and then got everything put away.

"All done. Now lunch?" Amy grinned at Heather.

Heather laughed, "Yes. Purple Pelican here we come."

Back in the car, we headed down the road and right to a building that once looked like a house. It was massive on stilts that painted purple with a large wrap-around porch and a back deck that went out over the water.

"Wow, this is not what I pictured." Heather said, as we climbed out of the car.

"It's exactly what I pictured." Denise said.

"Me too." I added.

"Flora was right about the purple. This is amazingly purple!" Amy laughed. "I love it."

Walking in, we were greeted by a friendly hostess. She couldn't have been much older than Olivia.

There I go, thinking of home again. I thought. *Stop it.*

I needed to check my text messages to see what my darling daughter had sent, but now was not the time as the hostess led us to the back deck to a table overlooking the water.

"This is perfect. Thank you." Heather said for the group.

"Your server will be right with you."

I looked out over the water. It was crystal blue, sparkling in the mid-day sun.

"This is amazing." I stared at the view.

"It really is," Denise agreed.

The other two were studying the menu. Denise looked at me with an absent look on her face. It appeared like she wanted to say something, but instead she picked up her menu. I stared at her for a moment. She'd seemed so distracted. Even at the airport yesterday, it felt like she was holding back a little bit.

I wanted to ask her what was on her mind, but it would have to wait until later, as our server came to take our drink order.

"I'll be right back with your drinks." He said.

"This redfish does sound good." Amy commented after he left. "What is everyone thinking?"

"I'm leaning towards the shrimp and grits." Denise said.

"Catfish platter." Heather said.

"So, I'm the only one who doesn't know?" I pouted.

"Looks that way." Amy laughed.

"Ugh, okay."

I skimmed the menu once again, settling on a soft shell crab platter just as the waiter came back with our drinks and took our order.

"I know you'll laugh at me, but I have to ask, when do we start the treasure hunt?" Heather asked sheepishly.

"Tomorrow. Today I plan to lie out by the pool." I said, turning my face to the sun. "I plan to go back with a nice tan."

"Same." Denise chuckled.

"Same, but with an alcoholic beverage in hand."

"Okay, so enjoy the sun today. Head to the church tomorrow. It's a *plan*." Heather emphasized the word plan and added a light laugh.

"Yes, this week is about relaxing with good friends." I smiled.

"No, great friends," Amy said, raising her glass. "To great friends."

"To great friends!" We repeated, then tapped our glasses.

"I can't believe how long we've been friends." Heather said, looking around at us. "Well, I guess Amy and I have been friends longer, but I'm so glad I met you, ladies."

"Same. So glad we met." Denise said.

"Thank you, Internet." Amy laughed.

"For real." I laughed.

"I miss those Friday night chats we'd have with the bigger group. Come as you are," Denise said.

"Oh, yeah, I miss those!" Heather added.

"I forgot about those. It was so much fun. Mommy chat nights after the kiddos went to bed," Amy said.

"I miss Donna."

"Aw, Donna."

She was a friend of our who had died suddenly of pancreatic cancer. It seemed to happen so fast.

"I'm glad I was able to go to her funeral." Heather said. "We had a good show of support from the group."

"I didn't get to go because I just had Ella and couldn't travel." I said.

"I wasn't able to go either." Amy said.

"I think that is when Sid had her ear tubes placed, if I remember correctly."

We continued to reminisce about folding flat sheets, vibrators, and dryer sheets. Our discussions were better than any Internet search and there was always someone available, day or night.

"I learned so much from our group." I added. "I couldn't have done half of what I did without everyone's support."

"Aw, I feel the same. There were some dark days for me, especially through my divorces." Amy sighed.

"Good times."

"Yeah."

"I would be lost without you all."

Chapter Sixteen: Denise

Lunch had been good, but I couldn't eat all of it. I brought my leftovers back to the house, but I wasn't sure if I would have time to eat them, given Heather's food schedule for us. She had brought us printouts of everything, including maps of the area with Xs marking different points of interest.

She was so sweet and cute to do that for us, and a little bit crazy. I loved her.

It was so nice to catch up and remember all the fun times with my dearest friends, including the ones not here with us. I wish we could plan a big group reunion like we used to, but it seemed like smaller group get togethers worked out better these days. When I had to travel for work, it was comforting to know that there was a friend available for drinks or dinner.

But I couldn't help but think of our friend Donna. What if I was next? What if in a year a group of our friends was sitting around remembering me?

I said a brief prayer for Donna and myself.

Then I shook the negative thoughts, because we were all getting changed to enjoy the pool. It was something I'd been looking forward to since we picked the house.

That was until I pulled out my swimsuit, that just a day ago I had felt so good about. Now I wasn't feeling extremely comfortable with my body, especially knowing what was inside of it.

"Damn body." *Damn cancer.*

But perhaps I was the one that let it down. I hadn't taken as good care of it as I should, shoving pizza and burgers into it for years, mixed with soda and not nearly enough water or vegetables.

Though my doctor said it could be something in my genes. That could be. I may never know, but I knew I needed to do better. Shrimp and grits were probably not the best choice. Though I had been doing better. This was vacation and it wasn't like eating a few extra green things now was going to kill the cancer.

I slipped into the swimsuit, then checked myself in the small mirror. Thank goodness for the tankini with the shorts and pleats strategically placed around the stomach. Even though I felt so fat and bloated, I didn't look too bad.

"Meh, that's as good as it's going to get." I grabbed a towel and went to join my friends outside.

Marissa was in a gorgeous two piece. The rest of us were in things a little more modest. Amy had a suit much like mine with shorts, but her top was shorter, which showed her stomach.

But I felt a lot more comfortable next to them than Marissa. She was the sweetest, but I was intimidated by her in a lot of ways.

She had a high-powered job, and her confidence was a ten. Her ability to command a boardroom and an entire company, she was my hero. If I could be anyone when I grew up, it would be her.

Amy was playing bartender.

"Margaritas for all." She said, handing them to us all.

"Now, this is what I'm talking about. My friends, the beach, a pool, and adult beverages." Marissa said, taking a long sip from her drink.

"Just what the doctor ordered." Heather joked.

My nerves were on edge. I flinched at her comment. My doctor had sort of ordered this for me. She wanted a relaxing time with my support system. That's what this was supposed to be.

I let it go and took a long, slow sip from my glass. It was a stalling technique, so I didn't have to talk, but nobody seemed to expect anything from me and they all leaned back in the lounge chairs.

For the rest of the afternoon, we laid back and soaked up the sun. No agenda, no deep conversations. Just friends enjoying a quiet moment with cold drinks and the sun.

At some point, Amy fixed us another round of drinks. She was the best bartender.

"I did it during college to make a little money. It was the best job. Sometimes I wish I could give up my day job to bar tend again." She confessed.

"You were the best." Heather confirmed. "Remember that one drink you had? What was it called?"

"Oh, the one with the cucumber and jalapeños? I just called it the Summer Sizzler, but it really wasn't something I made up. I can't remember where I learned it. I just couldn't remember the name. That's why I just called it the Summer Sizzler, which could be a real drink, too." She shrugged.

"You should make them for us," Marissa begged.

"I'll grab the ingredients next time we go to the store."

"I'm gonna swim a few laps." Heather stood and dove in.

After a while, Amy joined her. It looked cooling, but I didn't want to get in. Marissa and I simply watched.

An hour later, we started cooking dinner. My stomach turned a bit at the thought of eating, but I forced myself to eat at least some. I didn't want to raise eyebrows, and Heather's chicken looked and smelled so good.

"This is so good, Heather." Marissa said.

"Thanks. My boys used to love this chicken."

"How are they doing?"

"Oh, good. Tyler was accepted to law school and works part-time. Then Cody has an internship lined up for the summer."

"That's wonderful. I'm sure you're proud of them both." I said.

"What about you, Marissa? How are your kids?" Heather asked.

"All doing well, sort of. You know Jack was having trouble with his car, but he got that worked out. His college is going well. Emma is so independent that I rarely hear from her. It makes me a bit sad, but also so very proud, considering one of her sisters is the least independent person I know. Though Olivia is never afraid to speak her mind."

"Olivia is a lot like her mom." Amy chuckled.

"Touché." Marissa replied. "Her and Jackson are probably the most like me. Emma and Ella are more like Mike. Focused, calm."

"Sidney is nothing like me." I said. "But I don't really think she's like her father, either."

"Is she loving married life?" Heather asked.

"Very much so. I keep expecting her to tell me she's pregnant." I said with a smile, but I didn't add the rest of my thought which was if she didn't have a child soon, I may not get to see my grandchild.

The conversation shifted to Amy's children and then to work topics. Our company used Marissa's HR program, so it was neat to listen to her share about it. Amy was in computer programming, so they could relate stories.

A quick look at Heather made my heartache for her. She looked a bit lost in the shop talk, but I could see by her eager expression that she desperately wanted to be involved.

When there was finally a lull in the conversation, I took my opportunity to draw her in.

"Heather, what do you think our plan of attack should be at the church tomorrow?"

Her eyes lit up. "Well, I have been studying the map of the church. It shows all the windows and a description of each. I was thinking it would be an east facing window, because of the clue about the direction. What is right of the south, east, correct?"

"That makes sense." I said, smiling at her.

"There are roughly sixty windows that face the east, though, so it is still a lot to look at." She added.

"Well, the song to the west... is there a pipe organ or something musical?" Amy asked.

"Yes, a few, actually. In the main chapel and then there are two smaller ones where they host music concerts. I watched one on YouTube. It was beautiful. It was a trio of harps, but the pipe organs were in the background."

"Oh, I might have to look that up." I said.

"I'd like to watch that, too." Marissa added.

"Then we'll focus on those three rooms?" Heather asked.

"I think that sounds like the right plan. If we don't find something there, then we can expand our search." Amy said.

"I'm so excited about getting started." Heather giggled.

We finished up dinner after that, and I volunteered for cleanup duty. Amy fixed everyone a mixed drink and when I was done with the dishes, I joined them on the deck. The sky was just taking on the dusky color of night, but still light enough to see the waves rolling and crashing at the shore. It was so peaceful.

I sipped at my drink and soaked in the beauty of friendship and nature. I tried not to focus on what awaited me back at home or the turmoil that was happening inside my body.

"Do we want to play cards or something?" Amy asked.

"Yes! I'll go grab a deck of cards." Marissa got up and ran into the house, coming back with a deck of cards. "What should we play?"

"Hearts? Spoons? Or just poker." Amy suggested.

"I vote for hearts." I said.

"Sounds good to me."

We dealt out the cards and began. An hour later, we were laughing so hard, but the yawning started and my stomach was gurgling quite a bit. I needed to go take my medicine and lay down.

"Well, that was fun, but I'm going to call it a night." I said, standing.

"Yeah, me too. I haven't laughed that hard in a long time, but I'm beat."

We cleaned up, then filed in. I let the other ladies use the bathroom first, because I had a feeling I was going to need more time. I got a large glass of water, swallowing my pills, and then waited my turn.

"Oh, sorry, did I take too long?" Heather said as she exited the bathroom.

"No, not at all."

"Okay, good. Well, good night."

"Good night." I watched her walk to her room.

Chapter Seventeen: Amy

We pulled into the parking lot next to the church. It was about ten minutes before they opened to the public. There was already a long line outside that ran down one side of the building and around the back side.

This church was known for its intricate windows. The number and detailed pictures were among the best in the world. People came from all over to tour the facility, and they weren't all treasure hunters.

"What do we do until they open?" Marissa asked.

"I guess just... sit here?" I said, looking towards the church. I didn't want to stand outside. It was hot and sticky, and I didn't want to get all sweaty before walking through the crowded church, elbow to elbow with strangers.

"I'm so excited. I can barely sit still." Heather giggled. "I've been waiting for this moment for weeks."

"It's a beautiful church. I can't wait to look at all the stained-glass." Denise said.

"Just as long as we look go for the clue first, then we can sightsee." Heather added.

I suppressed a laugh. My sweet friend was such a stick to the plan type.

"Of course, Heather. We'll find the clue first."

"Not sure why we think we can find it so easily that we'll have time to sightsee." Marissa added. "The other teams have tried and failed, even after looking for a week."

"Perhaps they didn't know what to look for."

"And we do?" Marissa argued.

"Well, no, I guess not. I mean, the clue doesn't say what it is, but... I feel like I'll just know when I see it," Heather said wistfully.

Marissa's phone was going off. She was firing off messages one after the other, and mumbling to herself.

"Sorry, ladies, Jackson needs money. I never see the kid and now he needs money. Something about his car."

"Why isn't he asking, Mike?"

"Don't even get me started on that." She grumbled as a new text came in. "Ugh."

"Oh, it looks like the doors are opened." Heather said, pointing. The line that was outside was slowly moving in. "Time to treasure hunt!"

She hopped out of the car, barely waiting for the rest of us to join. This time I didn't suppress my amusement at my dear friend. She was like a little kid on Christmas.

She looked back to ensure we were with her, so we jogged to catch up with her. We then fell into the end of the line and shuffled along until we reached the front. Even though we'd waited in the air-conditioned car, I was sweating as we made our way to the front doors.

Heather pulled out her phone to present our tickets to the attendant.

"That's for the four of us." She said.

"Of course." The attendant scanned the code. "Enjoy yourself, ladies." He said with a nod as he handed us each a brochure.

Inside was a story of the church and of the stained-glass windows.

Each picture is a scene from the history of town, state, or from the Bible.

I already knew that from my research, but it was interesting to hear about. Inside, the church was packed with people. Maybe this wasn't the best time to come. However, the church's website had said it was always crowded, which added to the dificultly of looking at the windows for the clues.

There were always people trying to see or take pictures. In the online forums, there was a team that got into a huge fist fight with a tour group. They were all banned, which ended that team's run for the treasure, at least until someone solved this clue and shared the results.

We had already talked about not sharing any of the clues, except for when we had to register our find online to get the next clue. My understanding is that those were kept private.

It was the teams that bragged about their find that had given the first ones to others. That gave us a little head start, but we had no intention of telling a soul, at least not until we found the treasure, and even then, maybe not.

I looked around. Even in the entrance, there were massive stained-glass scenes. As my eyes focused and adjusted to the lower indoor light, I could tell this scene depicted Noah's Ark. It was beautiful, and the jewel colors dappled the room. I put my hand out to capture them in my hand. Even if we didn't end up with the treasure at the end of this, this moment was priceless and the colors were seared into my mind.

"It's hard to move forward." Heather whispered to me.

"Yeah, we may be at the mercy of the crowd on what we see." I whispered back.

"This first room is one of the eastern facing ones though, so we might be okay." Heather said.

I nodded, then relayed the information back to Marissa and Denise. We all put our game faces on as we moved with the crowd into the first room. We stepped in to find an enormous room, but could only see so far because of the crowd and the overhanging balcony above us.

"This is the smaller sanctuary and is used mostly for small weddings or funerals." Heather shared.

I nodded as I tried to see inside the room. The crowd had stalled, I'm assuming, so people could look and take pictures ahead of us. I could only get a peek at some pictures. I could see what looked like maybe Adam and Eve in the Garden of Eden. There was so much detail, all shaped and created with pieces of colored glass.

"The color is stunning." I whispered to Marissa, who was leaning around me to see.

"It is. I can't wait to see more." She reached back to pull Denise closer to us. "You have got to see this."

The crowd started moving again, but so slowly that it almost felt like we were going backwards. Soon the slow shuffle had moved us underneath a window labeled the Tree of Life. We turned in awe. Marissa pulled out her phone, pulling us all together quickly so she could get a selfie with the picture behind us.

I stared as best I could at each bit of the window, but I couldn't tell if there was a clue there. My guess was it wouldn't be in one of the Bible scenes, and more than likely when we got to the room with the city's story in it.

"This is massive. How are we supposed to find a clue in it?" Denise whispered to Marissa and I. Heather was a step or two too far to hear.

"I have no idea." I mumbled, staring up. "This goes on forever."

"Yeah, the clue could be at the top." Marissa said.

"Maybe we can see it from across the room better." Denise said.

Heather looked back at us, nodding her head for us to catch up. I smiled and joined her side. We walked the entire room, trying in vain to see something.

"Well, that room was a bust." Marissa pouted as we moved into a long hallway.

The hall had stained-glass windows on both sides, floor to ceiling. The church was laid out in a grid with larger rooms connected by these long hallways. There were more pictures than I could even imagine.

"Holy moly." I said, taking it all in.

"There won't be a clue in here since these aren't east facing." Heather said.

"Are you sure, though?" I asked.

"No, I guess it could be here." She looked around. "But I don't even know where to look."

We kept our eyes moving and trying to take it all in, as we slowly moved through this room and into the next sanctuary. It was even larger than the first room. Heather let us know this one was also used for weddings, but they did Sunday mass in here as well.

"The largest one is the last room we will go through and it is used for larger ceremonies like Midnight Mass or Easter Sunday Mass." She shared.

"You have studied up on this. It's been so helpful." Denise praised.

"I don't have much else going on." She laughed, but her eyes told a sadder story.

"We all appreciate it." I said, leaning over to hug her.

"Thanks. I'm just glad you suggested this."

We made our way through the hall into the next room. The crowd seemed to get larger, but I'm not sure how. It was difficult to get out of line to move around, so staying in one spot wasn't possible, because the others in line wanted to move forward. The crowd just moved as if drawn forward mechanically, like we were on a conveyor belt.

We just did the best we could to see the pictures and look for clues.

I looked up to see that we were under a picture of the Last Supper. It was so detailed that I almost forgot to look for clues, but I could now see why some teams took a week to look around and still had found nothing.

We moved into the last room. The one that Heather had said was for special ceremonies. This is where all the Florida history was.

"It has to be in this room." I whispered to Heather. She nodded, reaching for my hand. We held hands as we moved through, occasionally squeezing each other's hands in excitement.

"Oh, is that the Commodore?" She pointed to the one across from us. "He has been the key to everything so far, right?"

"You're right." I passed the message back to the other two, and we focused all our energy on that window.

Without knowing better what we were looking for, it was hard to tell. The window portrayed a nautical scene. It looked like perhaps the battle between the Commodore and the Pirate Claude de Palencia. It had to be in that picture.

I looked at every element, but nothing screamed at me. There were too many details to look at as the crowd pushed us forward and then out into the hallway.

"Ugh, this isn't as easy as I thought."

"Yeah, I thought it would be easy, but I guess the other teams were right. It's not an easy one." Heather said, squeezing my hand.

A few more hallways and small rooms that were more like conference rooms or classrooms maybe, before we made it to the end. There was an option to exit or walk back through.

"Do we try again?" Marissa asked.

"I wouldn't mind doing another lap," Denise said.

"It truly was beautiful and I wouldn't mind another look." Heather said.

"But look for the clue, too."

"Of course." Heather giggled. "You're starting to sound like me."

"Oh, no! I do." I laughed.

We walked back to the start and got in line. An hour later, we were no closer to the clue than the first time through.

"One more time and then lunch?" Denise asked.

"I don't know if it will do any good," Marissa said, crossing her arms hard.

"Well, this time, let's just take as many pictures as we can. Then later we can go through them." I suggested.

"You really are sounding like me," Heather said.

We all laughed, but everyone agreed to take pictures. We started from the beginning once again. We did nothing but take pictures of as many windows as we could. We took wide-angle shots and close up, trying to get as much of the details of the windows in each.

We reached the exit for a third time, and this time we exited out to the parking lot. We were quiet as we walked through the outdoor spaces. From here, the windows had a different look. Perhaps we were thinking of it all wrong.

"Should we try to look at the pictures from the outside?" I suggested.

"What? They aren't as detailed out here." Marissa laughed.

"That might be the key, actually." Heather said.

"Could work." Denise looked over at the building.

We began taking as many pictures as we could, especially those on the east side of the building. It was just as crowded outside as it was in, but we managed to move around okay.

After a lap around, we headed back to the car and Heather gave me directions to a burger joint we were going to try.

"It has good reviews online." She said.

"Sounds good."

"A burger sounds good."

"I want a cold beer."

I put the car in drive, taking one last look at the church before exiting the parking lot.

The first clue hadn't gone as I'd expected, but I probably should have known that's exactly how it would have gone. The church was a popular tourist attraction, and I had read there could be large crowds, but I thought the clue would scream to us.

Boy, was I wrong. We still had time to make this happen, but the time with my friends was priceless.

Chapter Eighteen: Heather

I bit into my burger, savoring the flavor. Melty cheese and earthy mushrooms mixed with the grilled onions to create a flavor explosion. At least something today was going right.

But we'd agreed to not talk about the treasure hunt until after lunch. I was okay with that because I was frustrated. I thought it would have been easier to find the clue, or at least that the windows would be easier to see. The windows themselves had not disappointed, though. They were gorgeous.

Still, I had faith that once we got to look through all our pictures, we'd find the clue.

"Oh, my gosh, this is the best burger." Amy moaned.

"The fries are amazing." Marissa said, dipping a fry in the secret ketchup sauce that was served alongside them.

"I was starving." Denise said.

I nodded as I took another big bite of burger. It really was the best I'd ever had. It was juicy and meaty.

I wanted so badly to talk about the church, but there would be time for that later. My friends would just laugh at me. I know it was with love, but I didn't want to annoy them either. It's what I did best, annoy them and act awkward.

"So are we doing beach or pool after this?" Amy asked.

It was a mix of answers.

"I'm not a fan of sand." Marissa said.

"There's that outdoor shower to rinse off." I said.

"But it gets everywhere." She laughed.

"Baby powder helps." Denise added.

"Really? Put it on before or after?" Marissa asked.

"After. You just dust a little on and the sand dries and comes off." Denise said.

"I don't have any, do you?"

"I do." Denise. "I always have it for the beach. It was a lifesaver when Sid was little."

"How did I not know this? I have four kids. I should have known this."

"I swear I thought I'd shared this tip before." Denise looked at all of us.

"I didn't know." Amy said.

"Me neither." I said.

"Well, dang, I guess you're never too old to learn something new." Denise smiled.

"Does that mean we are going to hit the beach when we get back?" Amy asked.

We all agreed, but Marissa added a quick stop at the liquor store again. So, with lunch done, we headed over to the spirit shop again.

"Welcome back, ladies." Flora was behind the counter again.

She was an interesting character. Grandma vibes but looking like an overcooked beach bunny. Today she had her hair in space buns. It was a youthful look, but somehow worked on her in her hot pink sundress with no bra.

"Thanks. Gotta get more booze." Amy laughed as she made her way to the vodka.

"Ladies after my own heart." She laughed.

I picked out a couple of bottles of wine. I wasn't sure I was going with mixed drinks today, but a glass or two or maybe three of wine sounded nice.

"Are you, ladies, having a good time here?" Flora asked when we got to the checkout.

"We are. Yesterday we hung out in the pool. Today we're going to the beach."

"Fun. I love the beach. I spend all my free time there."

No kidding. I thought.

I darted my eyes towards my friends, careful not to let my snarky thought show. Marissa was biting her lip and looking away. I guess I wasn't the only one who thought that. Flora was a sweet lady, but I wanted to give her an enormous bottle of sunscreen.

We finished with Flora and headed back to the house.

"Alright, ten minutes to get changed and then we hit the beach?" Amy asked.

"Actually, my stomach is bothering me a bit. I think I'll lie down for a while," Denise said.

"You okay?" I asked.

"Oh, yeah, just all the good food. I can't eat like a kid anymore." She chuckled.

"I understand that." Amy said. "Alright, beach for three."

I watched Denise closely, really hoping she was okay. There was something odd about her body language. She seemed tense, trying to be still. She looked a bit like when my boys lied to me.

"You sure?" I asked. "Do you want me to stay with you?"

"No, I'm fine. Really. It's just too much food. Go have fun." She smiled and then went to her room.

I shrugged and went to change. I'd brought three swimsuits. I had to rinse my first one out and then hung it to dry, but I would likely do a load of laundry before wearing it again.

I pulled on my new tankini with shorts for the bottoms. I noticed Denise had brought one like it, too. I loved it because it hid some flaws which I liked. I grabbed a fresh towel, a bottle of water, and my sunscreen.

Amy had the same thought, laughing when she saw my bottle.

"Gotta protect the skin." She laughed.

"Can you believe we used to oil up to go out?" I laughed.

"Yeah, burned to a crisp."

"Alright, ladies, I'm ready, too." Marissa said, bringing in her own bottle of sunscreen. "I guess Flora taught us something besides some drink recipes."

We laughed, but then slathered ourselves in the white lotion. I did extra on my face. I always burned there if I didn't.

With that done, we headed to the private path and across the street to the beach. It wasn't too crowded here. We had learned that this was not a public beach. It was for residents and guests only. That was nice because I didn't want to deal with a large crowd, not after the church today.

We found a nice spot, laid out our towels, and then settled in for an afternoon of nothing. I'd brought my tablet so I could read or play games. Marissa had her phone and Amy had a paperback book.

"Risky to bring a paperback to the beach." I teased.

"Yeah, well, I like to live on the edge."

We read in silence for a while, but after a bit, Marissa's phone started up.

"They can't even let me have one day." She sat up and checked her message. "They can't find mom's medicine journal. I have to call them."

She walked away from us to talk. We could hear her angry tone, but not her words.

I looked over at Amy with a shrug and a smile.

"Are we worried about Denise?" She asked before I got back to my tablet.

I sat up. "Did you notice she was acting a little weird, too?"

"Yes, she's been much quieter and usually she is the one drinking me under the table, but she's holding back a bit."

"I know. I'm worried about her. She seems to be on the edge of tears, especially today."

"I want to ask, but I don't want to pry," Amy said.

"Me neither. I guess we aren't as close as I thought we were." I looked over at Marissa, who was still arguing on the phone.

"I guess you and I are closer because we grew up together." She paused and studied me. "But I don't feel like we share as much as we used to."

My mouth dropped open, but I quickly closed it. "You think so?"

"Well, maybe I don't. I just take for granted you're there. That someone will be there." She sighed. "I don't know what I'm saying."

"No, I think I know what you mean." I bit my lip, trying to decide if I would share. "It's no secret that I'm lonely and bored without the boys to keep me busy, but… I've been looking for a job."

"Oh, that's wonderful. How's it going?"

"Not well. I'm feeling small and useless now." I could feel the tears forming.

"Oh, gosh, Heather. You are far from useless. Why do you feel like that?"

"I'm not qualified for anything. I have no work experience. At least nothing in nearly thirty years. Nobody wants to hire me."

"Their loss, truly. If I had a job, and we lived closer, I would hire you in a second. You are incredibly organized, thorough. You are the hardest worker I know. I mean, look at all the work you put into this vacation."

"That's because I have nothing else to do with my life."

The tears were flowing now. Her kind words touch the nerve. It was a relief to hear this person who I looked up to think so much of me.

"Well, I think it's more than not having enough to do, and more to do with you, all of you. You don't give yourself enough credit."

"Aw, you're the sweetest." The tears were really flowing now.

"Now if you don't stop crying, I'm going to be bawling right along with you." She choked and wiped a tear.

"What the heck did I miss?" Marissa said, coming back to find us both wiping tears and blubbering a bit.

"Heather was feeling sorry for herself, but I was telling her how wonderful she is."

"Why would you feel sorry for yourself?" Marissa actually sounded surprised.

I sighed, "I tried to find a job and… can't."

"Why can't you?"

"Because I'm not qualified for anything."

She eyed me for a moment. "Okay, I'm sure Amy already said this, but seeing all you did for this trip, you would be an asset to any company. Heck, if you lived closer to me, I'd hire you in a second."

"Thanks. I think I'm going to apply at the craft store when we get back. I just need something to keep me busy."

"What brought that up, anyway? I was only gone a minute."

"It was more like five, but I asked if we were worried about Denise." Amy said.

"Yeah, what's going on with her?"

"We don't know, but she just seems... not herself."

"I have wanted to ask her, but if she isn't comfortable sharing, I didn't want to push," Marissa said.

"That's what we said." I gestured between myself and Amy.

"I guess it was easier to bond over our children and the worries about them, not as much about us," Marissa said.

"Yeah, that's true." Amy said, looking at me. "I mean, we had deep conversations in the beginning as we were getting to know each other, but less over the years."

I looked at them. Two of my best friends in the world, but their words struck a chord.

"Maybe this trip is about finding more than the treasure. Maybe the treasure is... us," Heather said.

We stared at each other as we realized that was the truest statement of the trip so far. I was just the first to share my vulnerability with the others. It felt like a huge weight off my shoulders having that burden out there. It wasn't solved, but I felt better.

Chapter Nineteen: Marissa

After Heather's confession on the beach, we headed back. I had borrowed baby powder from Denise and left it on the back porch before we left, so we could dust off when we got back.

"Look at that. It works!" I said, as I was able to brush off the sand easily.

"Where has this trick been all my life?" Amy laughed.

"It could have saved my car from a lot of sand." Heather added.

We then went to get cleaned up and changed. It was my turn to make dinner. I was going to grill us some chicken breasts, then put it on salad. Something simple, but perfect for a hot day.

I headed to the kitchen to season the chicken and then set it to the side. Next, I wash and chopped the veggies for the salads. I added those to the bowls before taking the chicken outside to start the grill. When it was ready, I put the chicken on and then went into wash my hands.

Amy joined me.

"This looks good. Simple, but perfect."

"Thanks. I thought it would be nice after that heavy burger at lunch."

"Yes. Want me to fix you a drink?"

"Yes, thank you."

"Comin' right up."

She stepped over to the bar and I went out to flip the chicken. It was cooking nicely. When I came back in, I saw Heather had joined us. She had a glass of wine. Amy handed me a vodka with cucumber and fresh jalapeños floating in it.

"This is what I used to call a Summer Sizzler, but that was thirty years ago." She laughed.

I took a sip. "Mmmm. Love it."

I pulled the chicken. I let it cool a bit before slicing into it.

"Should we check on Denise?" Heather asked.

"Maybe."

"I'll go." Heather stood and started towards the bedroom.

"Sorry, ladies. I'm here." Denise said, coming around the corner. "I guess I was more tired than I realized."

"Great. Dinner is ready."

We all grabbed a bowl of salad, topping it with our own dressing, and then went to sit on the back deck.

"Such a beautiful evening." Denise said.

"It really is," Heather mused.

"We missed having you on the beach with us today." I said.

"Yeah, I'm sorry. I just needed to rest."

"You feeling okay?" I asked.

"Oh, yeah, much better after resting. I think the travel, then the heat, and the crowds of today, plus the heavy burger today, I just needed a break." She smiled and then looked down, busying herself with stabbing at her salad, then taking a big bite.

We let it die there as we all focused on our dinner, eating mostly in silence. Just a little friendly small talk sprinkled in between bites.

After dinner, Amy volunteered to clean up and the rest of us sat on the deck, enjoying the evening. We didn't talk about anything important, but the plan was to go through our pictures once Amy was back.

"How is the family doing?" Heather asked. "Did they find your mom's journal?"

"Yes, but now I'm worried they haven't been following it. Thank goodness for Ella. She's the one that realized it was missing. She is far too responsible for her age." I took a sip of my drink.

"Otherwise, things are okay, though? I know you were worried."

"Overall, yeah. Olivia is still not happy, but I don't think I'll ever make that girl happy." I shrugged. "I'm okay with it."

"What about you, Heather? How is Jason doing with you gone?"

"He seems like he's doing okay. He is pretty low maintenance, and I left him a bunch of pre-made meals. He just has to pop them in the microwave."

"See? Organized." I said.

"Yeah, but I still don't know how to translate that to a job. Nobody is looking for someone who packs her husband's meals."

"I feel like I'm missing some context here." Denise said, sitting forward.

"Yeah, beach side confessions. She is feeling down because she can't find a job. But she's brilliant, right?"

"Completely brilliant. Honey, I would hire you any day to be my assistant, if I were allowed one." Denise sighed. "Budget cuts. No assistant for me. I have to share with our finance department."

"Well, thanks." Heather said. "Almost makes me feel better, even if I could make the two-hour commute to you."

"Yeah, I guess it isn't comforting to say 'if I had...' instead of, 'I have... And, of course, the commute would suck." Denise laughed.

"Yeah, but I understand sentiment and appreciate it."

Amy stuck her head out. "Anyone need a drink refill?"

"Yes, please." Heather and I said. Denise declined. Heather and I exchanged a concerned look.

"My stomach is still a little full." Denise shrugged it off.

My phone chimed.

"Not now." I moaned as I pulled up my phone. It was just Mike sending some love and hoping that I was enjoying the trip. "Oh, thank goodness. Just Mike. Nothing's wrong. He was just sending love."

"Good. You deserve a break." Denise said with a smile.

"Should we look through our pictures?" Heather asked, waving her phone in the air.

"Yes, let's do it." Amy said, coming out with a tray of drinks. She passed the drinks to Heather and me, then took a seat.

We all pulled out our phones, adjusted our reading glasses, and started scrolling. I was in awe of the beauty of the church all over again.

"This Last Supper one is amazing. It was probably my favorite." Denise said, as she stared at the picture.

I pulled up mine, staring at the details of it. "It is exquisite."

"I knew there were a lot of windows, but wow, that was far more than I could have imagined." Denise said.

"Do we narrow it down to a collection?" Heather asked.

"I was thinking in that last room, the largest with the scenes from the battle." Amy said.

"Yeah, that's what you said when we were there. I took most of my pictures there." I said.

"Me too." Denise said. "Here is the first one I took."

She flashed us the image. It was the largest window with the battle scene in it. It was elaborate with flashy, jewel colors showed a battle. The center piece of the window was two ships in the heat of battle. Cannons firing, swords raised as a pirate is shown mid-swing over the water as he barrels towards the other ship. At the horizon was the coast. The white sandy beaches and the beautiful pines and oak trees that dotted the coastline.

"It's the trees! Or a tree." I blurted out.

"What?" Everyone yelled as they quickly scrolled to the same pictures on their phones.

"Oh, my gosh, I think you're right!" Heather gasped. "It makes sense. It is another thing that makes this area special. The oak and pine trees that grow here. That's why they called them out in the pictures."

"This is so exciting!" Amy squealed. "Who is going to log it into the website to see if we are right? Or really, if Marissa is right." She smiled at me.

"I think Marissa should do it." Heather said, turning to me.

"Are you sure? I know you have a lot put into this, too."

"No, it really should be you." She insisted.

"Okay." I pulled up the website on my phone. "Oh wow, this is so exciting."

I hadn't realized until that moment how important the treasure hunting piece of this trip was to me, too. Looking up at my friends' eager faces, I typed in the clue and included a couple of my pictures. It took a few seconds to process, but soon the clue was accepted.

"Congratulations! You have figured out the third clue. The next clue will be emailed to your entire team." I read. "Oh, my gosh, we did it!"

"Wow, I can't believe it," Heather said as she pulled up her email.

We read the next clue together.

As the battle waged on, the ship it did sink. Captured here on this quiet and quaint path, hung on the large and reaching. No one will see the truth or the sea.

"Alright, so we have to find a tree?" Denise asked.

"That's what it sounds like." I read it again.

"So, we go to the state park tomorrow. They are supposed to have the oldest trees in this part of the state." Heather shared.

"See, not useless!" I pointed out. "You have done so much research and you remember it all."

"I guess, but that doesn't mean I can get a job simply because I can remember a few facts." Heather frowned.

"Don't think like that!" I reached for her hand. "Put as much energy into your job search as you did this vacation, and I promise you'll get the perfect one for you."

"You're the sweetest." She leaned over to hug me.

We sat for a moment in silence.

"Well, tomorrow is planned. Yay!" Amy cheered.

We all laughed. It was the perfect tension breaker that we needed at that moment.

"To us!" Denise grabbed a drink.

"To finding another clue!"

"To wonderful friends."

"To not hearing a peep from my family."

Clink.

"I'm so glad that you suggested this trip." I said to Amy.

"I'm just glad you all could come. This has been just what I needed." She smiled. "Another round of drinks?"

"Yes! I'll take one of those summer things." Denise said.

"Well, okay." Amy stood, coming back a few minutes later with fresh drinks for us all.

"Another toast?" I asked.

We raised our glasses.

"To the PIMs!" It was the name of our online mom group. It stands for Psychotic Internet Moms. It was a joke, but it stuck.

"Yes, to the PIMs." Everyone yelled.

It was the perfect night with my best friends, and there was barely a peep from my family. Life was good.

Chapter Twenty: Denise

I had a rough night after eating too much fatty, rich food and having a few drinks to celebrate finding the third clue. It meant I spent quite a bit of last night hugging the toilet. It was miserable. Maybe I shouldn't have come on this trip, and instead, I should have pushed for the surgery and treatments to start sooner.

As I leaned against the cool, bathroom tiled wall, I pulled up the support forums on my phone. Reading through a few threads where others shared their stories it made me feel better and gave me hope. My journey was only beginning. Some of them were on the other side and could share their survival tales.

I still didn't know how or when I'd tell anyone else. It was on the tip of my tongue the last few days, but I just couldn't make the words come out. My friends were looking at me sideways, and I didn't know how much longer I could keep this from them, especially if they found me doubled over in the bathroom. Thankfully, none of them had woke during the night to find me there.

I washed my face and then went back to my bedroom as quietly as I could. If I could just get a little sleep before we started our day, I might be able to fake my way through yet another one.

A couple of hours later, I could hear the others in the kitchen. My stomach felt better, so I pushed up and headed back to the bathroom before joining my friends.

They had moved out to the back deck. It was becoming our favorite morning routine. Stepping out to join them, I inhaled the salty air mixed with the fresh coffee in the mug I was carrying.

"Good morning, ladies." I greeted.

"Good morning." They said.

"Are you ready for the day of clue hunting?" Heather giggled.

She was so into this, I almost hated for it to end for her. She was enjoying the trip and purpose of the hunt. It was adorable.

"I am, and I don't need to ask if you are."

"Ha, yeah, I'm so ready." She laughed.

"I have no idea how we will find a clue in a forest." Marissa said.

"Always being the realist in the group, Marissa." Amy teased.

"Hey, just trying to keep our expectations, mine included, in check."

"Oh, no. There is another team now here looking, too." Heather flashed us her phone, which looked to have the treasure hunting forum pulled up.

"Seriously?" Amy grabbed Heather's phone to read it. "Son of a... but it doesn't look like they have the church clue yet, so that's at least something."

"It's a bunch of college guys. They're our kids' ages." Marissa gaped at her phone as she read about the other team. "We can't let some kids beat us. We raised them... well, not them, but you know what I mean."

Marissa rarely got flustered. I hadn't realized how important this was to her. Like me, I thought she was just along for the ride. I smiled at her.

"Well, then we need to get a move on if we want to beat them." I stood and nodded towards the house.

"Alright, let's do." Heather popped to follow me into the house.

We all headed inside to get ready. I threw on some yoga pants and a tank top, put my hair into a ponytail, laced up my tennis shoes. I held my arms out, shook it to check my arm fat. I hated it, but I was with my friends today, so I would not worry about it. There were other things to worry about.

Putting a hand on my stomach, just to check its readiness. "Good to go."

Heading to the kitchen, I grabbed myself a water bottle. Marissa and Amy joined me.

"I hope we can stay ahead of this other team. I was so excited when it was just us looking." Amy said.

"Yeah, I thought it would be a breeze and we could spend more time on the beach." Marissa said.

"Well, a hike through the state park sounds fun." I said. I just hoped that there were bathrooms easily accessible.

"Sorry, ladies, I'm ready now. Jason messaged me, so I was replying to him." Heather said, coming into the room. She was glowing.

I was sometimes jealous of my friends' marriages. But after my marriage to Sidney's father, I had vowed not to be in another relationship. I'd dated a little, but nothing serious. Honestly, I was a happy single — most of the time. But seeing her blushing face as she spoke about her husband caused that lonely stir.

"Alright, ready to go Treasure Hunting Mamas!" Amy cheered.

"Let's roll."

With water bottles in hand, we headed to the SUV and then to the state park. Pulling up at the gate, the guard greeted us.

"Morning, ladies. It's a five-dollar fee to get in for the group."

"Each or total?" Amy asked.

"Total." He smiled.

She handed over the money, he handed her a map.

"Enjoy the park."

Amy steered the car forward and to the designated parking lot. The lot was about a quarter full, so that was good. We shouldn't run into too many folks on the trails.

"Looking at this, there are a dozen trails. With no sign of which path we should take." Heather said over the map.

"Well, we just pick one and hope for the best, I guess." I said as I looked over her shoulder. "Look, these two merge, so that would be our best choice to cover more ground, right?"

"But do you think they would put the clue on the most traveled path? Maybe one of these smaller ones." Heather pointed to one. "This one maybe."

"The clue said quiet and quaint." Marissa added.

"It also says no one will see the truth and the sea, so maybe this path that is going away from the beach. It looks like most of the others have some view of the gulf." Amy said.

"Brilliant!" Marissa said.

We hopped out of the car and headed to the trail that led us away from the gulf. It was a warm, humid day and didn't take long for the sweat to start, but it felt good to be alive.

"I guess we have to look at all the trees." Heather said, looking around.

"Will we even know what the clue is?" I asked.

"I think so, or I guess I hope we will." Amy said, stepping towards a large oak and running her hand along it. She then circled it. "Not sure why I'm looking so close to the trailhead. I'm thinking they would find one further back."

"True."

We walked on, enjoying the scenery. Birds were flitting around in the trees, tweeting and chirping back and forth to each other. A squirrel ran across the path, stared at us, and then ran up a tree.

There were several gnarly oak trees. I assumed it was oak and not pine because of the reaching part of the clue. Tall and thin was how I'd describe the pines.

This path appeared to not be popular as it was overgrown and in places nearly impossible to cross. If not for the trail markers along the path, I would have thought we had gotten off the track.

"This is wild." Marissa said as she swatted at an overhanging branch.

"Yeah, I guess this is the road less traveled." Heather laughed.

"Perhaps that's a good thing, right? Meaning we picked the right way," Amy said.

"Maybe so." I mused, looking around for anything that looked like a clue.

We came around a bend and the path opened up. There was a large, reaching oak right in the path. It was almost like a spotlight shone down on it and angels were singing.

"That's it!" Heather said, running to it.

We laughed and followed quickly behind.

"Now what?" I circled around it. Nothing jumped out.

"Maybe it's just the tree. Should we try putting a picture on the app?" Heather asked.

"We can try," Amy said, pulling out her phone. She snapped a few pictures, then pulled up the site. "Here goes."

She entered it, then frowned.

"Nope. It says you're getting warmer."

"Well, that's disappointing, but I assumed it wouldn't be that easy." Marissa said.

"Maybe something on or around the tree."

We spent the next hour searching high and low.

"Nothing. Just... forest debris." Amy said, kicking at the ground.

"Did we think it would be easy?" Marissa asked. Once again, she was the voice of reason here.

"So now what?" Heather asked.

"I guess we need to go back and rethink this clue." Amy said.

Everyone turned to go back, but something didn't feel right about just leaving. I pulled out my phone to take a few more pictures. I could look at those later.

"Taking more pictures?" Heather came up to my side.

"Yeah, I just have this feeling."

"Me too." She pulled her phone out and took a few at different angles than I was taking.

"Are y'all coming?" Marissa yelled.

"Yeah, just a sec." I yelled back.

A few more snaps later, we jogged up the path to catch up to our impatient friends.

"Club tonight?" Amy asked.

"Sounds fun." Heather replied.

We hiked back to the car. I couldn't get the nagging feeling that the clue was at that tree. I just didn't know what it was yet.

I stared out the window as we drove away.

"Should we stop for lunch or eat at the house?" Marissa said. She was driving now.

"Out." Amy said.

"Agreed." Heather and I added.

"I'll look for something." Heather said, already scrolling through her phone. "Oh, what about pizza?"

"Sounds good."

"Perfect."

"Great." But it actually didn't sound great. The cheese, bread, and fat were sure to upset my stomach. I'd have to be careful and only eat a little bit. I'd eat a salad and maybe a slice of pizza.

Heather gave Marissa directions to a hole-in-the-wall pizza joint. I wouldn't have given it a second look as the sign above it simply said: PIZZA, but the parking lot was nearly full.

Marissa pulled into a spot. "Wowzer. This doesn't look like the type of place you'd pick, Heather."

"It has excellent reviews, and for your information, I can be quite adventurous." She blushed.

"Oh, Ms. Heather, are you speaking about *in the bedroom*?" Amy teased.

Heather giggled, "Maybe. I'll never tell." She opened her door and jumped out of the car.

"That girl is full of mystery." Amy said, as she opened her own door. She caught Heather in a hug. They laughed. I watched my friends. This was the exact reason I wanted to come. The little moments of friendship.

"You okay?" Marissa asked. Neither of us had yet to exit the vehicle.

"Oh, yeah, just enjoying the trip." I gestured towards our two friends. "Stuff like this is the best."

"It really is." She reached her hand back to me. "I'm here, though, if there is something on your mind."

I smiled, squeezing her hand. "I really appreciate it."

We joined the others and went inside. The place was just as unimpressive inside, with its dark and dated decor, plastic tablecloths and wood paneling walls. The smell of oregano, tomato, and cheese had my stomach growling. Okay, I'd eat two slices, but that was it.

"Hi, welcome in. How many?"

"Four."

"Okay. It will be about a ten to fifteen minute wait."

"Great."

"Name?"

"Amy."

"Alrighty, gotta ya." The hostess smiled.

We stepped back against one wall to wait, but thankfully, we only waited a few minutes before we were seated.

"Welcome, have y'all been here before?" The server asked once we were settled at the table.

"First time." Marissa said.

"Do you have any recommendations?" Amy asked.

"Any allergies or dietary restrictions?" The server asked.

We all shook our heads.

"In that case, I'd recommend the cheeseburger pizza or the chicken spinach. Both are fantastic."

"Okay, thanks." Marissa spoke for the group.

We gave our drink orders, and then the server turned to get those.

"I'm thinking I'll get a side salad, too." I said.

"Oh, that's a good idea." Amy said.

"So, everyone get a salad and as a group, we split a large pizza?" Heather asked.

"Perfect."

We decided on the cheeseburger one. The server came back with our drinks, took our order, and then left us to chat.

"I'm mildly annoyed that we didn't find the clue today." Amy said.

"Me too." Heather frowned. "I was sure we could find it, but it was like finding a needle in a haystack."

"Or a very specific tree in a forest." Marissa chuckled.

I pulled out my phone and started scrolling through the pictures. Heather leaned over to look with me. We discussed each picture.

"Look at how the tree branches out. It's so big." She said.

"They are amazing."

We flipped through a dozen or so pictures before the salads arrived. I put my phone down to eat. The salad was huge, which was good. I could get full on veggies before the pizza arrived, but when it did, the smell had my mouth watering. It was topped with hamburger, cheese, pickles, onions, and chunks of tomatoes, then a special sauce swirled around it.

"Oh, yum," Amy said, as she put a piece on each plate. "Here you go."

I bit into the saucy, cheesy pizza and practically moaned.

"This is so good." I said.

"It is. Good choice on the restaurant, Heather."

"Yes, perfect choice."

"Aw, shucks." She smiled. "But, yeah, it's good."

We finished our meal, thanked the server, and then headed back to the house. The afternoon was spent by the pool. I enjoyed floating around the warm water and watching the clouds going by.

Later, we got all dolled up to go to a club. I hadn't been to a club in ages. Not since we all went on one of our larger group outings.

I smoothed the black dress over my curves, and then I studied myself in the mirror. Not bad. Despite eating poorly on this trip, I had lost a few pounds. I could get used to this.

I went out to join the other ladies.

"Are we ready?" Marissa asked.

"So ready!"

"I haven't been dancing in forever."

"Not since that group trip to Vegas."

"Oh, my gosh, Vegas was so much fun."

"And what about Baltimore?"

"With the exploding toilet?"

"I forgot about that!"

"So many wonderful memories."

We loaded into the car and headed to the boardwalk where all the clubs and bars were located. Marissa cranked up the radio. We sang along to every song. By the time we pulled up at the boardwalk, we were laughing and in the mood to dance.

"Alright, this one says they play 80s music." Heather pointed to one on our right.

It had brightly colored roller skates, cassette tapes, and a Walkman painted on the side. Music was thumping from inside. It was still fairly early in the night, only 9 pm, so the crowd was light when we stepped inside. After paying our cover fee, we headed straight for the bar, then found a table near the dance floor.

It was too loud for much conversation, so we mostly sipped on our drinks and did a bit of people watching. That's when I caught sight of a man across the room. He seemed to be watching me. He smiled and then swayed slightly as he began his journey towards me.

"If this thing between us is going to work, we've got to get one thing straight." He slurred out when he reached me.

"Hm, oh-kay?" My eyes dart to my friends' amused faces as they looked on.

"I don't work on January eighth."

"Okay." I had no idea how to respond to that.

"Elvis' birthday. I don't work on Elvis' birthday."

I burst out laughing. "Hm, no."

He stared at me, but then stumbled away.

I turned to my friends. "Y'all? What the heck was that?"

We laughed until we cried. After that, we just enjoyed the music, dancing, and a few drinks. It was a memorable night. One of the history books, especially the weird pickup line. I had a feeling I would tell this story for years to come.

Chapter Twenty-One: Amy

We had a blast at the club last night, but when I got back to the car, I had a bunch of texts from Scott. It started as checking on me, but it escalated quickly when I didn't answer him. He started accusing me of cheating, ignoring him, and several other things.

Scott: You were a whore when I met you, and you're still one

Me: I was out with my friends while on a trip, you know, about

Scott: But I haven't heard from you much, what am I supposed to think

Me: You can trust me. I love you

Scott: I love you too, but I hate being here thinking the worst

Me: Well talk to me instead of yelling at me

Scott: You yell at me for everything

Just as it seemed to be calming, he had to say something to set it all on fire again. We started hitting hard at each other and bringing in things that were irrelevant to the original fight.

He clearly was having a bad day and taking it out on me. It continued until we both were typing in all caps that we weren't speaking to the other.

I threw my phone to the other side of the bed, then cried myself to sleep. It really put a huge damper on the wonderful day I'd had with my friends, even if we hadn't found the next clue. We danced, we'd laughed, and had tasty drinks. Heather was our designated driver. She volunteered, which was generous of her.

But seeing the messages as we drove home sobered me right up, but I tried to hide it until I was alone. Crying in bed, I also missed my cat. He had been my constant companion through all the hard stuff, but also the good stuff. If he was here, he would be snuggled on my chest, purring.

Waking up, my eyes felt raw and puffy. I headed to the bathroom, gasping when I saw my face. It wasn't really a surprise after drinking, a late-night, and then all the crying after.

I splashed cool water on my face, which felt good against my irritated eyes and skin.

There was a knock at the bedroom door. I went out to open it.

"Yes?"

"Can I use your restroom? Denise is in the other." Heather asked.

"Um, yeah, I'm done." I tried to keep my face down.

"You okay?"

"Oh, yeah, I'm fine."

She studied me for a second, nodded, then closed the door to the bathroom. I breathed a sigh of relief that she didn't push me for details.

I headed into the kitchen to start the coffee going. While I waited for it to brew, I pulled out my phone. I hadn't had the guts to look at it yet to see if Scott had sent anything.

Scott: Sorry about last night. I love you.

I sighed. He always thought just a simple apology was enough. I wanted him to acknowledge that he hurt my feelings, not just being sorry, but the *why* was he sorry. If I pushed, it would start another fight.

I simply replied that I loved him, too. He sent back a heart, and I gave a smile face. This went on until I was giggling.

"That's a better face than the one I saw when you answered the door." Heather said, coming in.

"Oh." I jumped. "Yeah, mornings, am I right?"

"Mmm, I guess." She studied me for a moment. "Alright, if you don't want to share, I'm not going to push you."

She gave one more look before grabbing a mug. I hesitated only a moment, but it would feel really good to talk to someone. She was one of my oldest and dearest friends. I knew she wouldn't judge me.

"Okay, fine. Scott was mad last night that I wasn't answering his texts. We got in a huge fight."

"I'm sorry. Things good now?"

"Well, better, but honestly," I took a deep breath, "Things haven't been great. We fight all the time. All the time."

"I'm sorry."

"Thanks." I could feel tears forming. "I don't want to fail in another... marriage."

"Oh, sweetie." She threw her arms around me. "You aren't a failure. It happens."

"But why does it *keep* happening to me?" Tears were flowing now, both for my sadness and for her show of kindness. She was a dear friend.

"I can't answer that. It really just is."

"Thanks, but..."

"What's going on in here?" Marissa asked, joining us.

I wiped at my eyes. Heather smiled.

"Sorry, just a rough morning." I said, trying to smile.

"I gathered that. Wanna talk about?" Her tone was sweet as sugar and it instantly put me at ease.

"Scott and I got into a huge fight last night."

"Oh, Amy, I'm sorry. You okay?"

"I guess."

"Are you sure it was just a fight, not more?"

"Yeah," I sighed. My throat tightened. "No, it's more. I think... I think we're going to end up getting divorced."

Marissa didn't say a word, just stepped forward and wrapping me in her arms. That simple gesture caused me to start bawling. She rubbed my back and started whispering soothing, comforting words. Heather joined us in the hug with tears streaming down her face.

"What the heck?" Denise said, coming in.

"I might be... I might be getting divorced." It got a little easier to say.

"Oh, Amy." She joined the group hug.

These were the best friends a girl could have. I didn't even know if we were getting divorce. I hadn't contacted a lawyer, but I'd thought about it. Having been down this road before, I knew it well. I didn't even need a map this time. It was just a matter of time before he knew it, too.

It hurt my heart to think of actually divorcing him, though. I truly did love him and wanted this to work out, but I hated the fighting. It was piddly, stupid stuff. We couldn't even have a normal conversation without it turning ugly and us yelling at each other.

"Have you thought about counseling?" Heather said after a few minutes.

"Not yet, but maybe that's the next step for us."

She had a point. We hadn't even tried that yet, but I was scared to suggest it. Did he think our marriage was as much of a mess as I did? If he didn't, what would he think if I suggested counseling?

"What would you tell any of us if we were in your shoes?" Marissa asked.

"I don't know."

"Well, I do. Do you remember what you said to Rebecca about her marriage?"

I sighed, "Can you imagine him with someone else? If you can without pain or jealousy, then it's time. If you can't, then there's still hope."

"And?" She smiled.

I thought for a moment. Could I picture Scott with someone else? Picturing it, my chest tightened and a lump formed in my throat.

"I can't. No, I still love him." A few tears fell. "I know, I need to work on this. Thanks so much for that. You truly are the best." I smiled wiping my eyes.

"Actually, that is all you." Marissa smiled. "I remember when you said that to Rebecca. I was at a low point in my marriage too, and that told me everything I needed to know about myself."

"Oh, I didn't know that. You and Mike were having trouble?" Heather reached for her hand.

"Yes. We were just starting my business. Four young kids, going in a million directions. It was just a lot of life changes at once. Instead of pulling together, we were pushing apart." Marissa nodded towards me. "Amy's words made me stop and reevaluate my life and feelings. I talked to Mike and things got so much better. It was communication that we needed."

"Until recently?" Amy said it as part question, part statement.

"Yep, until recently. I'm burned out and need to talk to him again. I have just been trying to overcompensate for so long and it enabled everyone else to become lazy and dependent on me."

We sat there quietly for several minutes. All lost in thoughts, not looking at each other. I pictured Scott's face, his voice, his thoughtful gestures.

I knew in my heart; I didn't want a divorce, but I also didn't want to fight. Communication was the key. Isn't that basically what Marissa said?

Thanks to their kindness and shared tears, I was feeling a lot better. We all looked at each other at the same time, wiped our eyes, then laughed together.

"Y'all really are the best. I'd be lost without you."

"We love you." Heather said, reaching for my hand.

"And we're here for you anytime you want to talk about things." Marissa said.

"We definitely have your back," Denise said.

"Should we get fresh coffee and try to catch the sunrise?" I peeked out the window. "It doesn't look like we missed it yet."

"Yes!"

We all grabbed coffee and headed out for our morning routine. I felt lighter, more relaxed, sharing my worry. I should have known they would support me and not think less of me, even if I ended up being a divorcée again.

"Last night was fun. Did you all have fun?" Heather said, breaking the silence.

"I had a blast." Marissa said.

"I can't remember the last time I'd been to a club. It was so fun," Denise said. "But that guy!"

"Oh, my gosh, he was a hoot."

"He really likes Elvis."

"Apparently."

"So, should we make our plans for clue hunting today?" Amy asked.

"Heather and I took all those pictures. Maybe we should look through them again?" Denise offered.

"Sounds good."

We started scrolling together through their pictures, examining each one.

"This tree can't be seen from the sea. It's large and reaching. It has to be the clue." Heather said.

"But we already put it on the website and got a big, fat no," Marissa said.

"We still have the trail map. Why don't we go back through it?" I suggested.

"And I'll pull up the state park's website. We can look through pictures. Maybe something will stand out there," Heather said.

"I'll make us some breakfast while you all gather stuff." Marissa offered. "Wanna help me, Denise?"

"Sure."

An hour later, we had eaten and were combing through the pictures on the park's website, comparing them to our own, and going through the map marking landmarks.

"Oh, no. Those kids figured out the church clue! Now we are even." Heather gasped.

"Shit." Marissa said. "I lose to my kids all the time. I don't want to lose to kids I don't know."

We laughed, but it fueled our fire to try harder. With my head clear from marital drama, I hoped I could focus on the treasure hunt more. We had our game plan, now to get out there and find it.

We disbanded and got changed for the day, then packed up water bottles and snacks to take along. An hour later, when we pulled up to the park gate, the guard greeted us.

"Back again, ladies?" He smiled as he took our payment.

"Yes, it was so beautiful yesterday and we didn't get to see everything." I said.

"Are y'all looking for the treasure too?"

"Too?"

"Yeah, a group just came into look for some treasure."

"Oh, yeah, did they say which trail they were taking?" Heather leaned over me to ask.

"No, but I warned them and I'll tell you. No digging in the park. We can't have holes everywhere."

"Of course. We are just looking for a clue. It shouldn't involve any digging. Just looking around." I offered with a smile.

"Well, good luck. Between you and me, I'm rooting for you, ladies." He winked.

"Thanks!" we yelled as I drove forward.

It was only a quarter mile to the parking lot and the start of all the trailheads. We already had our plan. There was one other path that moved away from the sea, but when we first looked at the map, it looked like it didn't. We figured it out after looking through various online sources and comparing pictures.

There were a few cars in the lot, but no people, so we didn't get to size up the competition.

"Alright, Treasure Hunting Mamas, are we ready?" Marissa clapped as we headed to the trail.

It was a humid day with clouds in the sky, meant we could get rained on. But there was a gentle breeze and nice shady under trees, so both helped with the heat.

"I hope it doesn't rain." Heather said, staring up.

"It rains a little every day." I laughed.

It was true. Each day there was a quick down pour around 2 pm. When we were at lunch one day and made a comment to the waitress, she laughed and said, "That's Florida for you."

Today it looked like it might not just rain this afternoon for a few minutes, but possibly all day. Honestly, I welcomed the break from the heat.

As we walked, an older couple passed us on their way back to the parking lot. They smiled, and we all did a polite greeting, but we didn't see any other people.

"I wonder where that other team is?" I said, looking around and trying to hear anyone ahead of us.

"No telling. This is an enormous park."

"Hopefully, they're on the wrong path."

"Meaning, we're on the right one?"

We checked a few of the trees as we walked, but we were looking for a specific one that was supposed to be on this path. It was over a hundred years old and from the pictures; it had knots and reaching wide branches.

"Is that it?" Denise asked as we came to a fork in the road.

Unlike yesterday, this tree was in the dense forest still, not an open area. It spread above all the underbrush and looked like it held many secrets to the past.

This had to be it. I thought as we walked closer. I took my phone out to take pictures.

"This has got to be it." Heather said, also taking out her phone. "Lots of pictures, right?"

"You read my mind." I said.

While Heather and I took pictures, Denise and Marissa looked around the tree.

"I still do not know what we're looking for." Marissa said.

"Well, well, well, what do we have here?" A male voice came from behind us.

We turned to see four college-aged guys walking towards us. This must be the other team.

"Do you really think you can find the clue before us?" The tallest of the guys asked, laughing.

They looked twelve to me, but then again, everyone younger than me looked twelve now.

"Shouldn't you boys be in school or something?" I snarked.

"Shouldn't you be in a nursing home?"

"Ha, that's the best you've got?" I laughed.

"Nah, but I don't want to confuse you."

"Have you ladies found anything interesting?" Another one asked.

The four of us shared a look. There was no way we were going to tell them.

"No, we're thinking it's not this tree." Marissa said with such confidence, I almost believed her.

"Oh, really? You wouldn't just be saying that, so we'll look elsewhere?" The sharp-tongued one asked.

"No, we were just about to move on ourselves." She said. She nodded her head as if we were really going to move along.

"Nice try, but I think we'll have a look around," Snarky guy said.

They started moving around, peeking in the brush and tangles around the tree. One of them shimmied up the tree and began checking in the nooks and crannies of the tree branches. We watched from the safety of the ground.

Huddled together, we whispered about our next move.

"Do you move on?" I asked the group.

"Maybe."

"I think we have enough pictures to go through."

"I don't feel like watching them root around for the clue."

We started to walk away when the guys started shouting at each other.

"The boomers might be right. It's not here."

"What a waste."

"Let's move on."

"Later, ladies."

They moved on down the path loudly. I didn't even get to correct them. We're Gen Xers, not Boomers.

"Well, that's convenient. Do we keep looking here?" I was positive it was here.

"They just climbed all over the tree and didn't find anything." Marissa said.

"Yeah, but they didn't seem extremely observant. Heck, listen to how loud they are?" Denise pointed down the path.

"I say we move on." I said, "Who's with me?"

"I'm with you." Marissa stepped towards her.

Denise looked at me, but then nodded as she moved to join the other two. Only Heather hesitated.

"Come on, ladies, we are so close. I can feel it. It has to be here." She said. Her eyes were glassy with tears.

"Heather, it's okay. We'll find it." I said.

"But you don't understand. This… this is all I have. I have nothing else." She started bawling. My friends stepped forward to wrap their arms around me.

"You don't have nothing. You have us."

"We love you."

"And you still have your family. They aren't gone, just doing their life like you raised them to do."

"I just feel so useless. This was my chance to do something… something that was meaningful and for me."

"We are still doing this." I said, rubbing my back.

"Yeah, we just want to try another spot. We can come back to this one." Marissa said.

Her breathing became more even as she relaxed.

"That's it. That's it right there."

She pointed to a spot that was almost like a knot, but as our eyes focused on it, it was clear what we were looking at.

"Is that a rope?"

"Is that where they hung the pirate?"

"Oh, that's morbid, but kinda cool."

I snapped a picture, then I pulled up the website. The processing felt like it took forever. My friends leaned over to wait as the ship's wheel spun.

"Congratulations, you have found the fourth clue. The next clue is *'The war was won, so we took up the watch to keep the peace. The people safe until the end of the night.'*"

"Uh, my gosh! We did it." I squealed, but not too loudly. We looked around.

"Quick, let's get out of here before the other team comes back." Marissa said.

As we turned to head back down the path, the sky opened up. We laughed out loud as we ran for the parking lot. We reached the car out of breath but laughing and soaking wet.

"I can't believe we did it." I said. I reached back for Heather's hand. "I'm so glad you stopped us from moving on."

"I'm so embarrassed, but glad it worked out." Heather laughed.

I couldn't believe it, but we were still further than any other team so far. It was unreal. I wanted to pinch myself. It only took both Heather and I having breakdowns today to find it.

Chapter Twenty-Two: Heather

We drove away from the park, looking over our shoulders as we did.

"No sign of the frat boys." Marissa said once we were back on the highway.

"I can't believe we've done it." I said, giggling.

"Well, we haven't found everything yet, just one more clue." Amy said.

"But it's more than any other team so far."

"True."

"It's still fairly early in the day. Do we try to figure this out and go hunt for it?" Denise asked.

"I think so."

"Definitely."

"Let's do it."

"Okay, so the clue is '*The war was won, so we took up the watch to keep the peace. The people safe until the end of the night.*' Does that sound like it might be something at the fort?" I asked, reading it from the email.

"Hmm, yeah, maybe. Because they thought the battle was won when they hung the pirate, but his men came back to kill the Commodore at the fort."

"Yes! That's got to be it."

"So, we go tour Fort Aston?" I asked.

"Yep."

I gave Amy directions as we made our way over there. I could barely sit still as we drove across town to the fort. The city was named for the fort which made it another popular tourist attraction, but we found it not to be crowded on this day.

Amy parked in the nearly empty parking lot.

"Oh, we got lucky to be here during the middle of the week, I guess. Not many people here." Marissa said.

"It's ten dollars a person." Heather said, as we made our way to the ticket booth.

"I gotta ya, ladies." Amy said. "Four adults." She told the ticket taker.

"Okay, forty dollars."

Amy passed her card through the window. The lady ran the card, smiling at us.

"Here you are." The lady behind the window said. "And here is a map. It has all the information you'll need to know about the fort. Enjoy your visit."

We stepped into the fort. I fought the urge to squeal and start running through it, but that wasn't in my nature. I was just excited. We had found two clues, and I'd been worried we wouldn't even find one.

"That grin." Amy nudged me.

"I'm just excited. I can't believe we found two of the clues."

"I know. It's awesome."

"Okay, so what are we thinking here?" Marissa stuck her head between me and Amy.

"Well," I pulled out the map. "The sleeping quarters is where this part of the story takes place, so I'm thinking we head that way."

I pointed towards the west side where the men would sleep. The Commodore and his wife had a separate area, but it was in the same general area. We walked through the stone walls, taking in the sights on our way.

"Look at this view." Marissa said.

"It's amazing."

The fort was situated so that it overlooked the crystal blue water of the gulf. There was a mix of palm trees and pine trees along the outsides of the fort with a couple of large oaks inside the fort.

We read some placards as we walked along.

"Oh, look at this. It talks about the hanging."

"What are these numbers?"

As I looked at them, something told me they were important.

"Maybe we should take pictures of these." I said, pulling out my phone.

"Oh, good idea."

"Are you thinking it might by some kind of cryptogram?" Marissa asked.

"Yeah, I think so. I noticed it on the last one we passed, but it only just clicked." I went back to the last plaque and snapped a picture. "Okay, got it."

"Okay, so do we have to get a picture of all of them?" Denise asked.

"Yeah, I think we should. Then we can go back to the house and sort it out. Right?" I asked, looking around to see if they agreed.

"Yeah."

"Makes sense."

"Alright."

"I know it's hard, but it isn't supposed to be easy, right?" I tried to sound encouraging.

"You're right." They agreed.

We got busy finding the informational signs and taking pictures of those with numbers on them. They didn't all have numbers, so that was helpful. It made this go quicker. Two hours later, we had taken nearly twenty pictures and had seen every inch of this crumbling fort overlooking the gulf. The last home of Commodore Aston.

"Alright, ladies, ready to head back to the house for some decoding and lunch?" Marissa said, jumping into the driver's seat.

She and Amy had been our drivers for the week. I really appreciated. I wasn't comfortable driving in an unfamiliar city.

"Yes, ma'am!" Amy cheered.

"I'm starving."

"Thanks to you and Amy for driving us."

"Oh, of course, sweetie. We are happy to do the driving. Right, Amy?"

"Yes, of course." Amy smiled at me.

"We both appreciate it." Denise added.

We got back to the house and got sandwiches, chips, and drinks together for our late lunch. We chatted about the fort, the treasure, and all things Florida as we ate.

"I can't wait to figure out this clue."

"I know."

"Are you still feeling useless? You figured out that the clue was in the numbers." Marissa said to me.

I felt my face warm. "You keep pointing out all these things. It definitely helps my ego, but doesn't help me translate that to a job."

"Fair enough, but I just hate that you feel so bad about yourself. You really are incredible."

"Aw, I love you, my friend."

"Love you, too." She blew me a kiss.

"Well, I'll get the lunch stuff cleaned up." Denise offered.

"I'll go grab my notebook and a couple of pens." I said.

"Wait? You have a notebook and multiple pens with you on vacation?" Amy chuckled. "Of course, you do."

"You know me. I'm prepared for everything." I skipped off to retrieve the items.

Coming back to the kitchen, they had cleaned the table up and Amy was at the bar mixing us some drinks.

"We need drinks to work, right?" She said as I came back into the room.

"Makes sense to me." I replied as she handed me a drink. I took a sip. "Yum. What's this one?"

"I don't know the name. Pink Lemonade, club soda, vodka with a splash of lime juice."

"It's good."

"Thanks."

I grabbed another one to help her carry to the kitchen table, then handed it to Marissa.

"Why thank you, ma'am." She took a sip. "Oh, Amy, I think this is my favorite drink so far."

"Yeah? I like it, too." Amy said, taking a sip.

"Is there one for me?" Denise said, coming to the table.

"Right here." Amy handed her one.

"Oh, yes. This is good."

"Alright, now that we all have a drink, let's get started." Heather said.

"Yes, mom." Amy stuck her tongue out at me.

"Mature." I stuck my tongue out in reply.

"How should we attack this?" Denise asked.

"I'm thinking first. We just go through and get all the numbers written out. Then we have to figure out if they did a straight up cryptogram where A equals one, B equals two, etcetera. Then, we have to unscramble it to make a message. That's what we'll put on the website to claim the clue."

"Maybe you and Amy work on getting the numbers down. Denise and I will look for different codes, just in case it isn't a straightforward one."

"Smart. Okay, Amy, you good with that?"

"Yes, ma'am." She grabbed a pen. "You sort through the pictures and I'll write."

Thirty minutes later, we had all the numbers down and had assigned them each a letter based on the first thought on the code.

"Drink refill, anyone?"

"Yes!" Everyone yelled.

"I'll come help you." Denise said.

Marissa and I each took a blank page, then started trying to unscramble the words. I was normally great at word puzzles.

"Maybe I should send the letters to Cody." I mumbled.

"Not a bad idea. Didn't you say he was good at puzzles?"

"Yeah, almost scary good."

She stopped writing and looking up at me. "Send it to him."

I laughed and then took a picture of the letters.

"Wait? Is this cheating?" I asked, my finger hovering over the send button.

"Yes, but so what? You think other teams aren't using lifelines? Besides, you made him, so he's part of you."

I thought for a moment, "Can't argue with that."

I hit send, then we sat back to wait. Amy and Denise brought us a second drink.

"What's going on?" Amy said.

"I sent the letters to Cody." I giggled.

"Will he write back? My boys are so bad at that." Amy chuckled.

"He can't resist a puzzle."

My phone chimed. "He's in!"

"Well, way to go, Cody." Marissa cheered.

"I say we go sit by the pool until we hear from him." Denise said.

"Agreed."

We grabbed our drinks and headed to the deck. The clouds of the morning had cleared. Thankfully, we dried from the morning rain by the time we were done at the fort, and it hadn't rained on us again.

"Look a pelican." I said. It was flying past when we came out.

"Oh, that's so cool."

We took our seats and watched the pelican. Another joined it, as well as several seagulls. From here, we could also see the people at the beach. My eyes found a young family. I watched the little children toddle around, jumping with excitement and trying to dig in the sand.

"I miss having littles." Amy mumbled.

"Me too." I admitted.

"I love them about age five." Marissa said.

"I only had the one, so every stage was my favorite." Denise smiled.

"Aw, and she's a special one." I said.

"Thanks." Denise grinned. "I do hope for a bunch of grandbabies, or at least two."

"Any talk from her and Max?"

"Not yet."

"Well, Amy is going to have a grandbaby soon. When is Hannah due again?"

"Four months. It's crazy to think. My baby girl is going to be a mom."

"Does she know what she's having yet?" Denise asked.

"No, they have said they don't want to know, but I tried to tell them that I want to know." Amy chuckled. "She just laughed at me and changed the subject."

"I don't know if I would want to know." Marissa said. "I was surprised with all of mine, except Jackson who made sure it was obvious on the ultrasound."

"My Aiden did that too, but I did want to know, so it was okay." Amy said, laughing.

My phone chimed. "Cody did it!"

"What's it say?"

"Aston Memorial Gardens Cemetery."

"Oh, my gosh. Thank you, Cody." Marissa yelled.

"Thank him from all of us!"

"Yes, thank you, Cody."

I typed in the message, and he replied: **Good luck, ladies**.

"Oh, how cute."

"He is the sweetest."

"What a sweetheart."

"That's my boy. I knew if anyone could figure it out quickly, it was Cody."

"You should do the honors of submitting the clue."

"Are you sure?"

"Yes!" They all agreed.

I pulled the website up on my phone, typed in the clue, and attached a few of the pictures for proof that we were there. I watched the ship's wheel spin as it processed our submission.

"Congratulations. You are almost at the end. You're final clue. Oh, my gosh, y'all, we are at the last clue." I giggled and kicked my feet. "Sorry. The clue has been sent via email to each member of the team."

"Got it."

"Me too."

"The last clue."

A last goodbye and a rest for the weary. But caution and stony statue and query.

"So, are we all thinking that it is the cemetery?"

"Yes."

"Sounds like it."

"Definitely."

"Okay, so we have solved three clues in just a few days. One more to go."

"We should get dressed up and go to a nice steakhouse."

"Oh, maybe that one I told y'all about," I suggested. "Reardon's Steak and Seafood?"

"That works for me." Denise said, looking around at the other two.

"Yeah, I'm in."

"I have the perfect dress."

We jumped up to start getting ready, taking turns in the shower and bathrooms. It was time to celebrate, as we had plenty of time to find the last clue and then the treasure. While I waited for my turn in the shower, I checked the forums to see if the other team had made any progress.

They hadn't found the tree clue yet. I did a little dance.

"What's that little dance about?" Amy said, catching me.

"The frat boys haven't found the tree clue yet."

"Oh, yes!" She put her hand out for a high-five.

"What are we celebrating now?" Marissa said, coming out of the bathroom.

"Frat boys are stuck on the fourth clue."

"Yes! Even more to celebrate. Who's turn in the bathroom?" She pointed.

"Oh, mine." I jumped in.

I was so happy to be on this trip, but while I stood in the shower, it hit me. This trip was going to end in just four days. I didn't want it to end. I would go back to nothing.

Chapter Twenty-Three: Marissa

We celebrated the fourth and fifth clue by going to Reardon's Steak and Seafood. It was a tablecloth and candlelight place. I wore a black slip dress, backless with strappy stiletto heels.

The girls were all dressed similarly elegantly. Amy in red, Heather in a deep green, and Denise in black, like me.

"Hello, ladies, welcome. Have you dined with us before?" The waiter said asked.

"No, our first time." I said with a smile as my eyes skimmed the menu.

"Well, welcome in. Can I start you off with something to drink? We have lovely house wines. A red and a white."

We all ordered the red and then reviewed the menu.

"I'm thinking of a big ole steak with a side of shrimp." Heather said. "I usually only do a small steak, but today calls for a reward."

"I'm thinking lobster." Amy laughed.

"The steak with shrimp sounds good to me," Denise said.

"Great, so I'm the only one who can't decide?" I chuckled. "I'm usually the decisive one of the group, except when it comes to food."

Our server brought our drinks and dropped off a complimentary crudités plate for us. It was zucchini, celery, beautiful grape tomatoes, and carrot sticks. I grabbed a tomato, my weakness. It was earthy, sweet with a slight tartness at the end.

"Ready to order?"

Everyone placed their order while I skimmed.

"And for you?" The waiter got to me.

"Ugh, everything looks so good, but I guess I'll do... Sea bass."

"Perfect. I'll get this put in and bring out your salads in a few."

He turned and left.

"I still can't believe we did it." Amy said. "Should we toast?" She held up her wineglass.

"Yes." Heather said.

We all lifted our glasses.

"Here's to friends and family who know us well but love us just the same." Amy said with a laugh. We tapped our glasses.

"I'll add this to those who have seen us at our best and seen us at our worst and can't tell the difference." I said.

We laughed.

"Good one." Denise said, as we all clinked our glasses again.

"I can't think of one..." Heather said.

"I got one." Denise said. "It is around the table that friends understand best the warmth of being together."

"Oh, nice." I said.

"Here we go. Salads." The server, Asher said as he set them down in front of each of us. "Can I get you anything?"

"No, we're good." Amy smiled.

"Great."

We dug into the crisp, fresh salads. Halfway through, my phone chimed. Olivia had been blowing up my phone for days, but my reply was usually to ask your father or work it out. But often, I simply ignored her.

I continued eating until my phone chimed again. I groaned and looked at the display.

"It's Ella. She almost never needs me." Not like everyone else.

I read the text.

Grandma fell. We're at the hospital.

"Shit. My mom had an accident. I need to go call." I jumped up, running to the front door as I pushed Ella's number.

"Mom?"

"Yes, how's grandma? Do you need me to come home?"

"No, no, everything is okay. She's getting x-rays now."

"What happened? How...?" My mind was going in three million directions at once.

"They said her blood pressure was too high, she was complaining about being dizzy."

"Was she taking her meds?"

"Grandpa wasn't sure. He hasn't been keeping track well. He couldn't even tell the EMTs what she was taking." Ella said with a sigh.

"Alright, tell them I'm coming home."

"No, mom, we've got it. Grandma is going to be okay, and I'll handle her medicine from now on."

"But you have school, dance, homework. She has to take some during the day."

"We have Friday off, then you'll be home on Sunday. She'll only be alone with Grandpa one day before I'm home. It'll be fine until you get back."

When did she turn into me? I had always thought she was more like Mike, but now I was thinking perhaps she was me. I didn't want her to fall into the 'I will just handle it myself' mindset like I had. She needed to be a fourteen-year-old kid for a bit longer.

"You shouldn't have to handle all that. You're just a kid. Enjoy being a kid."

"Mom, seriously? I can do this." She said. "Oh, dad wants to talk to you. Here."

"Marissa, hi. I'm so sorry. I should have been watching them better. I should have known he wasn't giving her medicine on time."

"It's not your fault." I said, but honestly, I wanted to scream at him.

"I will make sure they do better." His heavy sigh was loud. "We depend too much on you. I need to step up and be in the moment when I'm at home."

"Oh, I haven't made it easy on everyone. I try to just handle everything. I need to learn to delegate and say no more."

"Well, don't worry about anything. We will handle this and anything that comes up. You just enjoy your trip."

We hung up, and I stood there a moment frustrated, wanting to run home, but knowing that would do no one any good. The point of this trip, besides the treasure part, was to give myself a break and make my family realize all I do for them. I think they were learning, but at the expensive of mom falling.

"Damn it." I muttered, then turned back into the restaurant.

I arrived as our entrées were being dropped off, which didn't allow me to update my friends until the wait staff left. Asher asked if we needed anything before excusing himself.

"Everything okay?" My friends asked as soon as the server was gone.

"No. Mom fell because they haven't been staying on top of her med schedule. She was getting x-rays. They'll call me back with the results later." I wanted to cry or scream in frustration.

"Aw, I'm sorry to hear," Heather said, reaching for my hand. "I'm sure she will be okay."

"That's awful, but I'm sure she will be okay."

"Y'all are sweet to say that, but I'm starting to regret my decision to leave them. It's too much for them to handle. I usually just do everything and they didn't know how or what to do. I should have delegated more, so I could leave guilt-free."

"Yeah, you do usually, but this is your chance to have a break. Take care of yourself." Amy said firmly.

"You've been burning the candle at both ends for so long, you don't even realize how much you handle and how much you could delegate." Heather added.

"How do you expect to continue to care for everyone else when you have nothing left in your tank? You can't pour from an empty cup," Denise said.

I looked around the table at my friends' concerned faces. They weren't wrong and that had been the whole point of this trip, but it was mostly to teach my kids that I wasn't their taxi service or their ATM. It wasn't to put my mom in harm's way.

Though dad should be able to handle his own wife's care. Except for a few minor aging related health issues and the recent UTI, he was a healthy man. It shouldn't fall on me.

"You're right. You are all right." I dropped my shoulders. "Okay, okay, I'm going to try not to think about it. They are all old enough and smart enough to handle this."

I tried really hard to not think about home, but I did. I could just picture my poor confused mother wondering where she was and what was going on. It broke my heart to not be there with her.

"This steak is incredible." Heather said.

"Mine too." Denise said.

"My shrimp is good," Amy added. "What about your sea bass?"

"It's excellent, but this asparagus is my favorite."

"My broccoli is steamed perfectly."

"What am I going to do about my mother?" I moaned.

"Aw, I thought you weren't going to think about it." Denise said.

"I tried, but if only I would hear an update from them."

"I'm sure you will hear soon. Those things always take time." Amy said.

We finished up dinner and ordered desserts to go. It would be a fun treat on the back deck when we got back to the house.

"A glass of wine, a game of cards with dessert, and good friends. That sounds like the perfect night."

We all agreed with Amy.

As we were heading out of the restaurant, my phone chimed.

Broken wrist. She's good otherwise.

"Just a broken wrist." I informed them as I replied. "A pain med and a soft cast."

I sighed with a relief as I read Mike's full message to my friends.

"Well, there you go."

"Not awful, right?"

"Hoping that she has a quick recovery."

I simply smiled and nodded to my friends.

Maybe they do have this. I needed to let go and give them the opportunity to do things for themselves.

We headed back to the house, changing out of our fancy clothes and into comfy pajamas. Then we took our dessert on the back porch. Amy grabbed a bottle of wine, I grabbed glasses, Denise got the deck of cards, and Heather got some forks.

Once we were all settled, I looked around again at my beautiful friends. They were the best a girl could ask for.

"I'm so thankful for you, girls." I said. "I wouldn't have been so calm about mom's fall without you."

"We love you."

"You're always here for me, us."

"You're amazing."

"Y'all are sweet, but I mean it. This hasn't been easy for me, you know, to get away. I don't slow down enough to think about it, but now that I have, it is too much for one person." I paused. "I think I'm going to let some things go."

"What are you going to let go?"

"I'm going to push Olivia to get her license so she can be more independent. I'm going to hold my dad more accountable for mom's care. I'm going to work less. I might, and I can't believe I'm going to say this, step down as the CEO."

"What?" they all blurted in near unison.

"I don't know yet, but it's been on my mind a lot lately."

"That's huge."

"Are you sure that's what you want to do? That company is your baby."

"I know, but Ella is trying to step into my shoes and while I love the go get 'em attitude and work ethics. I don't want her to burnout before she's even made it to college."

They nodded and agreed that it shouldn't be her job.

"I'll start with making everyone in the house step up more, but the next thing will be me stepping back from my job. By this time next year, I may only work part-time.

"Well, I hope that this vacation gives you the clarity you need," Heather said with a smile. The other two piled on with words of support and love.

They were truly the best friends a girl could ask for. I did not know what I was going to do, especially when it came to mom's care. It was too much to think about now.

Chapter Twenty-Four: Denise

After a night on the town and a gigantic piece of cheesecake washed down with two glasses of wine, my stomach was completely upside down. I ignored it as long as I could, but finally I could take it no more and I knew my stomach was going to give up.

I excused myself while my friends continued to chat and play cards.

I barely made it to the restroom before my stomach heaved. The contains of my stomach emptied. When it was over, I laid back against the wall, trying to breathe.

"Evil stomach." I mumbled. Was it too much to ask my body to just let me enjoy one night?

I knew my issues were more than just the tumor blocking my intestine, but was also age related. I couldn't eat like I used to. Rich, fatty foods for days were wreaking havoc on me.

I cursed as my stomach churned. It was going to happen again, but I tried to relax and breathe through it. Thankfully, the feeling passed, and I leaned back again.

There was a knock at the door. I knew someone was going to come check on me, but I hoped for more time.

"Denise, you okay?" It was Heather.

Like me, she had always been a caregiver. It was likely why she felt so lost in life now.

"Yeah, I'm fine." But as I spoke, my stomach called me a liar. It let loose more wrath on me.

"That doesn't sound okay." She said.

I tried to speak, but my stomach churned.

"I'm coming in."

"Noo…" But I hurled myself over the toilet seat again. I was at the dry heave stage, which was painful. I moaned, darted my eyes up to judge Heather's reaction. Her face was etched with concern.

"Oh, sweetie." She got a washcloth, running it under the water, then placing it on the back of my neck. "Want me to get you a glass of water?"

I shook my head.

The cool cloth felt so comforting. My body immediately relaxed, my stomach calmed, and I let myself fall back against the wall again. The wall and I were becoming one in this fight.

I mouthed thank you.

She smiled and sat next to me.

We sat like that in silence for several minutes. The only sound was my slightly heavy breathing and the water in the toilet as it finished filling back up. After a while, she stood without a word, taking the cloth from my neck and running it under the cold water again.

"This always helped my boys when they were sick." She said, putting back on the back of my next once again.

"Thank you." I whispered. "Too much good food."

"Yeah, I understand. I have a bottle of anti-acids in my room. I've been popping them like candy." She chuckled softly. "Would that help?"

"I have some, but not sure I'm ready." My stomach threatened again. I closed my eyes as I waited for the feeling to pass.

"Okay, well, I'm here for you." She sat back down next to me.

"You don't have to stay with me."

"It's no trouble."

I put my head back and let my body calm further. I hated to put her out. She should be enjoying the evening with friends, not babysitting the sick one. I don't know how long we were sitting alone before there was a knock at the door.

"You guys okay in there?" It was Amy.

"We're okay. We'll be out in a few minutes." Heather smiled at me. "When you're ready."

"Okay."

"I really appreciate you sitting with me." I said after Amy left. It meant so much to me. I wasn't alone.

"Not a problem. That's what friends are for."

I stared at her. That hadn't been my previous experience. I was the caregiver, not the one being cared for. Nobody had ever been there for me, even my ex-husband, when I was pregnant with Sid. He rarely went to the doctor's appointments with me and almost missed her being born. I'd done most of the laboring alone.

Then, over the years, I had to depend on myself or Sidney. We were Team Bennett Ladies. We just handled it between the two of us. She grew up faster than I wanted as she helped me around the house, made dinners, and cared for herself while I worked. But it made us closer.

"I think I'm feeling better." I flushed the toilet once more just to ensure it was good.

She held her hand to help me stand up. I let her. All her actions had me questioning my view on not telling my friends. Perhaps I should.

"I have colon cancer." I said it before I could stop myself.

"Oh, Denise." She put her arms around me. Her hug felt safe and loving. We began sobbing as she rubbed my back.

"Hey, y'all okay in there?" This time, it was Marissa.

I half-laughed, letting Heather go so I could open the door.

"Yes, sorry, I had eaten too much and it upset my stomach. I'm better now." I looked at Heather. "She was nice enough to sit with me."

"Why are you both crying?" Her tone was fraught with concern.

"I will tell you and Amy together." I gestured to leave the bathroom.

They followed me out to the deck, where Amy was texting. She looked up and smiled.

"About time y'all come back to the party."

"I found them crying in the bathroom. She says she'll tell us why once we were all together." Marissa said, crossing her arms as she took her seat again.

"Yikes, sounds serious." Amy set her phone on her lap. "As the kids say, spill the tea."

"Well," I looked at Heather for strength. She reached for my hand. I nodded. "I have colon cancer."

"Oh, Denise." Amy stood, wrapping her arms around me.

"Wow, I'm so sorry." Marissa came over to hug me, too.

The tears started to flow. Heather stepped into the house, returning with a box of tissue. She passed it around. Seeing them, I started laughing as I grabbed three.

"I haven't even cried this much in weeks."

They moved their chairs closer to mine, and we got into it. They wanted to know everything. I couldn't blame them for being curious. I'd been holding out on something big.

"Why didn't you tell us sooner?" Marissa asked.

I sighed. Suddenly, all my reasons for not saying something sooner really did seem ridiculous. Telling Heather had given me the courage to say it again.

"It sounds silly when I think about it, but my mom used to burden everyone with her illnesses and actually any kind of drama in her life. I didn't want to be that person. You all remember when she was in hospice, right?"

"Oh, I remember. I was ready to fly over to tell her off on your behalf." Amy said.

"Aw, I love you."

"You know you're not your mother, right?" Heather said in a firm mom voice.

"Yes, but I'm just so used to handling things, caring for her, being a single mom, and not having someone to depend on." I sighed.

"But you have us, friends, people who love you."

"Have you told Sidney?"

"Not yet."

"When were you going to tell her?"

"Um, honestly, I was hoping when I was in remission." I said sheepishly.

"What? No, you have to tell her."

"Tell her."

"She'll be so hurt if you wait too much longer."

"You're right. You are all right."

I looked at their concerned faces. I really should have told them and Sidney sooner, but I hated being a burden. It really was a silly reason. The doctor told me to talk to my support system, and I'd ignored her advice.

Sidney was going to be so hurt that I didn't tell her sooner, but I just hoped she'd understand. Her grandmother had been the source of many conversations over the years, so I'm sure she would get that part of it.

I tried to keep up as they continued to grill me, taking turns asking me questions.

"So, what stage are you? What are the doctors saying?"

"Stage three."

"Are you having surgery?"

"Yes, in about two weeks."

"Did you postpone it because of the trip?"

"No, they couldn't get me in sooner."

"Do you have someone to take care of you while you recovery from surgery? Drive you to and from?"

"Um, honestly?"

"Yes!" they all shouted.

"I don't. I haven't told anyone until today. It might be shortsighted, but I didn't think I'd need anyone." I held back the part that I thought about taking a ride share to and from, but it was only a passing thought.

"Well, look no more. I'll come stay with you. I can drive you to and from, then take care of you afterwards." Heather smiled brightly.

"I couldn't ask you to do that."

"You aren't asking." Her face brightened.

"Okay." I smiled.

"That's why you've been a little off this trip?" Amy commented.

"Yeah, I was trying my best to hide it. I wasn't sure if I wanted to share or not."

"Well, how'd that work for you?" Amy said with a laugh. "You can't keep important stuff from your friends."

"Your best friends." Heather added, taking my hand. "We love you and want to be here for you."

"We are your biggest fans, Dee." Marissa added, taking my other hand.

"Y'all are the best friends, for real." I wanted to laugh and cry. "Now, I just need to figure out how to tell Sidney and Max."

"We can't be there when you do, but we will be with you in spirit."

"Yes, we've got your back."

"You know she loves you."

"Thank you, ladies." I paused. "I'm just so scared about my future. Will I be the second in our group to pass away?"

"No, you're a fighter."

"You've got this."

"Don't talk like that. You're a survivor."

With my cancer news out there now, I felt lighter. It was an enormous secret to be caring around, and I should have told them sooner. I wouldn't make that mistake again, but now I had a support system in place and, according to my doctor, that just upped my odds of survival.

Chapter Twenty-Five: Amy

"So, is that it? Everyone got their secrets out?" Marissa asked.

"What secrets do I have?" Heather asked.

"You felt like a loser, but we got you straight on that, right?" I pointed at her.

"Oh, right. I'm over that. I'm going to take care of Denise and then just take it one day at a time after that."

"Good."

"And you're good with Scott, not good?" She asked me.

I studied her as I thought of her question. I really didn't know yet. We hadn't gotten to talk much, a few texts after that fight, but we haven't talked on the phone at all.

"It feels good to have talked to y'all about it, but I haven't gotten to talk to him yet. I feel like knowing what he's thinking and feeling will help."

"Makes sense."

"Marissa?"

"What about me?" She faked being offended, causing us all to laugh.

"You said you wanted to stop enabling your family, overcompensating, and you want to step back a little from your job," Denise said.

"Yeah, I think I'm going to do both of those things. My family really needs to step up and be more responsible for themselves. I mean, I know mom and dad need help. Ella can't drive yet, so she can only do so much at this point. But I'm determined to get Olivia behind the wheel. She can then take her sister places."

"Good plan. And work?"

"I honestly don't know exactly what that will look like yet. It's my baby, but it has a good start and will continue to be successful whether or not I'm there. I just don't know what I'll do with my time. I actually love being busy."

"You and me both." Heather chuckled. "But maybe we can figure out how to keep ourselves occupied together."

"Deal."

"I'm so glad we took this trip, and I don't even care if we find that last clue or the treasure." Amy said, sitting back. "This was just what I needed."

"Me too."

"I agree."

"The best trip ever."

"But speaking of treasure, tomorrow we go to the cemetery?" Heather asked.

"I think so." I smiled. "Last clue."

"And only a few days of vacation left."

"It has been a little easier than I thought it would be."

"I wasn't sure we were going to get that tree one."

"And I don't know if we would have figured out the cryptogram without Cody." Heather said.

"True. He was a huge part of our success to this point." Marissa raised her glass up in a toast to Cody.

"We would have figured it out, but definitely not as fast as he would." I said.

"True." Everyone agreed.

We were quiet after that. I'm not sure what the others thought about, but I was reflecting on our vacation and my time away. It had really opened my eyes to my problems, or honestly, lack of problems. I needed to loosen up and relax when it comes to Scott. He loves me and I do love him. More than anyone. He was different from other men in my past.

"I'm going to go to bed. My stomach is a still iffy." Denise said.

"Oh, good night."

"Night. Hope you feel better."

"Good night."

"I'm going too," Marissa said, stretching.

"I guess this party's over for the night." I chuckled, looking at Heather.

"Yeah, we have a big day tomorrow."

She picked up an extra glass left behind, a few napkins, and a plate. I watched my friend for most of my life. She was amazing. I wish she could see it.

"I love you, Heather." I said before she went inside.

"Aw, I love you, too." She smiled.

My mind flashed back to my little friend from kindergarten. Her smile was the same, just in an older, wiser face. One that has had a beautiful life raising two handsome, intelligent boys. We have shared so many laughs and so many tears over the years. I couldn't imagine life without her.

"I'm so glad we are doing this treasure hunt together."

"Me, too." She stopped at the door, turning back. "Why so sentimental all of a sudden?"

"I don't know. This trip just has me all up in my feelings. Or maybe it's just middle age."

She walked back, sitting across from me.

"I understand. With the boys gone, my life has gotten slower. I have more time to think and remember. I had hoped this trip would be a distraction, and in a way, it was, but it also had me facing how … things. How I got here, choices I've made, and really questioning my next steps. I mean, even more than before this trip. At least at home I could be in denial, thinking 'after the trip', but the trip is almost over."

"I understand. Me, too." I reached for her hand. "You are an amazing person. You're smart and I'm sure you will figure it out. You've always landed on your feet. Remember when your parents divorced, you thought that was the end of the world?"

She chuckled softly, "Yeah, it felt like it, but it turned out that they were so much happier and in turn were able to better parent. It wasn't always perfect, but they got to a good place, as did me and my sister."

"And you will now. Your boys are doing amazingly and that's because of the parent you were, you are."

"And you know Scott loves you?"

"I guess."

"You probably don't know this. I know I never told you and I assume he hasn't, but on the day of your wedding, he pulled me aside. He told me how lucky he felt. He knew you were guarded, that you'd been hurt, especially with Carlos."

I laughed. "Carlos nearly had me writing off men completely."

"But then you met Scott."

"But then I met Scott." I repeated.

"I don't know what's going on with the two of you, but I promise you can get through it."

"How do you know?"

"Because I've known you most of your life. I have been there for all your relationships, including all three marriages. This is the best one yet. You just lost hope somewhere."

My throat tightened as I felt almost as if my heart grew. She was right. I loved Scott more than anyone.

"Thank you." I whispered. "I really needed that."

"And I needed you to give me your pep talk." She stood. "This trip has been so much more than a treasure hunt. It's been about us. Each of us as a woman, a mother, and a friend."

With that, she walked into the house. I could see her through the window as she moved around the kitchen. She was right. This trip started as a treasure hunt and to take a break from life, but we were all finding a deeper friendship and a deeper understanding of self.

I fidgeted with my cell phone for a moment until I saw Heather had left the kitchen; I pulled up my texts.

You awake?

I held my breath as I waited for his reply.

Yep.

I hit the dial button.

"Hey, beautiful. What's with the late-night call?" His deep, sexy voice caused my stomach to flip-flop. Gawd, I loved that man.

"I just missed you and we haven't had time to talk."

"We've had time to fight." His tone tickled me. Normally, I would have gotten defensive, but tonight, I knew he was teasing me.

I laughed. "True, and I'm sorry for my part in those."

He chuckled, "Yeah, me too. I hate fighting with you."

"I hate fighting with you, too."

"So, we're good?"

"Yeah, I've had time to think and I... love you so much."

"I love you, too."

"When I come home, I'll try harder not to be so bitchy." I choked a little as tears formed.

"You aren't—"

"I am, and you know it." I half-laughed, half-sobbed. "I'm going to try counseling for myself."

"Well, I'll try not to be such a dickhead, and I could benefit from a little therapy myself." He laughed.

"So, it's a deal?"

"Yeah, babe."

We continued to talk, just small talk, married people stuff. He told me about his latest project at work, and I told him about our trip.

"Y'all are so close. I'm so proud of you."

"Thanks. I really had my doubts, but this has gone faster than I thought."

"Well, you're all smart ladies."

"Ha, I guess." I didn't want to admit to anyone outside of our circle that we used a lifeline to Cody.

"Archie misses you. He sleeps in the guest room most nights."

"Aw, I miss him too."

"I'm looking forward to having you home. Sunday evening, right?"

"Yep, just a few more days."

"Good luck, baby. I'll be sending good thoughts."

"Thanks. Good night. I love you."

"I love you, too."

With that, we hung up. I felt lighter than I had in months. That was the best conversation. I knew we would be okay now. I smiled, inhaled the salty night air, then went inside to go to sleep. Tomorrow was going to be a big day, or so I hoped.

Chapter Twenty-Six: Heather

Tonight had been full of deep conversations, laughs, and tears. It brought us all closer, or at least I felt closer to them.

After my heart-to-heart with Amy, I went in, cleaning up as I made my way to bed. I seemed to always be in mom mode, even among my friends. I laughed at myself.

As I headed to bed, I stopped at Denise's door to listen. I wanted to ensure she was sleeping and not feeling sick. It sounded quiet, so I continued on to my room.

It was at that moment I realized my purpose in life was to have someone or something to take care of. My love language was caregiver.

"It makes total sense." I mumbled as I snuggled under the beachy themed blankets and drifted off to sleep.

I woke with a smile, but then frowned when I realized I missed the sunrise. Sun was streaming in. Then I smiled again because I had slept solidly all night. The first time I felt so relaxed in months.

"Darn it." I sat up, quickly heading down the hall. First stop, the bathroom, and then to find my friends and coffee.

"Hey, y'all. Sorry I'm up late." I said, stepping out onto the deck.

"Hey. We didn't think you were going to join us today." Amy teased.

"I was about to go check on you." Marissa laughed.

"Rough night?" Denise chuckled.

"Ha, yeah, a bit." I could feel the hangover as my head pounded and my stomach churned. "I didn't realize I drank so much."

"But you remember last night, right?" Marissa laughed.

"I do." I looked at Denise. "I won't forget what I promised you."

"I appreciate it, but I still can't ask you to come stay with me."

"I want to and you didn't ask. I offered."

She simply smiled.

"We were just talking about the last clue."

"Oh, yeah?" I sipped my coffee.

"I checked the hours. They are open starting at 7 am and close at 8 pm."

"No rush then." I sat back with a sigh.

"A little rush. Those frat boys are on the fort clue now."

"Darn it, really?" I sat forward, pulling out my phone, and checked the treasure site website. "They are, but it will take them some time to get through that one, right?"

"That's what we were talking about. Plus, we haven't announced exactly which clue we are on. Only the administrators or whatever for the site know what clue we are on."

"That's true." I sighed. "It makes me feel a little better."

Once again, I relaxed back in the chair. I heard my friends chatting around me, but I just kept my eyes closed, taking in the sounds and smells. Despite the hangover, I smiled. This had been the best trip.

My phone beeped.

"Oh, it's from Cody." I announced. "He's checking to see how it's going."

"Aw, that's so sweet."

"What a sweet guy."

"What did you tell him?"

I typed up my reply and read it as I did.

We are going to the cemetery today to look for the last clue.

He sent back a thumb's up and a clover.

"Does that mean good luck?"

"I think so."

"I always ask my kids what stuff means."

"Seems like it."

"He so rarely texts me, but this gives me hope we will find it." I said. "He does love me."

"Of course he does."

"It sometimes feels like they've forgotten about me."

"I know that feeling," Amy said.

"I wish mine would forget me sometimes." Marissa laughed.

"You don't mean that." I gasped.

"No, not really, but they can be so needy. Just once, I'd like them to take initiative for their own lives."

"True."

"I'm going to make us some breakfast." Denise said, standing. She went into the house.

"Does she seem okay this morning?" I whispered.

"Yeah, maybe a little tired like the rest of us, but okay," Amy said.

"It's so sweet of you to offer to stay with her." Marissa said.

"I don't mind. It helps her and gives me a purpose, at least for a bit." I smiled.

We sat quietly for a while, before Denise came out to announce breakfast was ready. We went into find a whole spread.

"Is this French toast?"

"And bacon?"

"Plus, sliced fruit."

"Yes, only the best for my girls."

We ate and chatted, planning out the day. After breakfast, I cleaned up while the others went to get ready. Once I was done, I got showered and dressed. I sent Jason a text message.

Wish us luck. Last clue today.

He didn't reply right away, but I knew he would. He was likely at work already. I checked my reflection in the mirror before joining my friends. I couldn't explain it, but I felt different. Nothing had really changed in my life, but doing this treasure hunt and being here with my friends, I felt focused again, grounded.

I could hear Amy in my head cheering me on. Marissa saying what a badass I was. I giggled at the thought. I didn't curse, but she did and it made me feel rebellious thinking of saying it.

"I'm a badass." I whispered to my reflection.

I pictured my beautiful friend Denise and what the next months would hold for her. Thankfully, she was only a few hours away and I could easily drive to her. With no other responsibilities, I could stay with her any time she needed me. That made me smile more.

"I am a badass." I said, a little louder.

"Yeah, you are!" Amy said from the doorway.

I jumped and then laughed out loud, "Oh, my gosh, you startled me."

"I don't think I have ever heard a cuss word come out of your mouth. What would your mother say?"

"Ha, my mother curses. I don't know what happened to me, it just felt... wrong."

"Well, I like it." She threw her arms around me, kissing my check. "Now, come on, we have a treasure to find."

I laughed, grabbing my stuff, and following her to the car. We chatted and giggled our way to the cemetery. As we neared it, we sobered up.

"Wow, this is gorgeous."

The wrought-iron fence and large archway looked like it was straight from a horror movie, but in a beautiful way. It was an enormous property with ancient looking headstones. Some had intricately carved statues on top.

The landscaping was amazing.

"Look at these oaks. They are huge." Amy said as she steered the car into the parking lot.

The cemetery asked that all guests come to sign in. It was free to tour, but they asked for a donation. We signed in and then dropped ten dollars each.

"Wow, that's very generous of you, ladies." The older gentleman said as he handed us each a brochure. "Enjoy."

"Thank you."

We stepped out into the humid mid-morning air.

"Okay, this includes a map of the various historic sites." I pointed out.

"Good. It is likely the Commodore's that we are looking for, right? I mean, that's obvious."

"Obviously."

"But I'd love to look at some of the other grave sites. Like look, this one says 1899." Denise pointed to one that we were passing.

"Oh, that one is a child." I looked down. It had a sweet angel statue carved on top of it. "Only a few years old."

"They didn't have great health care back then."

"That's true."

We walked solemnly through the graves, stopping to read and honor those dead. We finally made it to the grave of Commodore William Aston and his wife, Henrietta Smythe Aston. They had two sons that were buried nearby.

There wasn't anything that stood out. It had their names along with birth and death dates. Not much else.

"Well, now what?" Amy said, looking around.

I skimmed the brochure. There had to be a clue here as to what we were looking for.

"The pirates are all buried here, too." I blurted when I got to that part of the pamphlet.

"Really?"

"No way!"

"Where?"

I pointed to the map and then looked around to orient myself. "Yep, over that way, I think."

"Let's go."

It was quite a trek to the far side of the property where the pirates were buried, and it was a warm, humid day. At least the shade offered some relief from the sun.

We walked down the perfectly manicured path, taking in more graves. We got to a section that was more recent ones. The headstones here, while beautiful, did not have the ornate beauty of the older markers.

As we reached the far side, the landscape wasn't as beautiful or well-kept. The headstones were smaller and less elaborate.

"We must be getting close." Amy said.

"Yeah, this section looks... I don't know, less cared for?" I said.

"It's a sad reality that this must have been more of the pauper side," Marissa added.

"Sad reality indeed." Denise said, squatting down to read one of the poorly written markers. "Hazel Williams, beloved wife and mother."

"This one says John Matthews. Brother and son. Died at thirty-five."

We read several more before we found a sign with skull and crossbones on it. It read, *"Here lie the outlaws and pirates that terrorized the Gulf of Mexico."*

"Oh, exciting." I squealed as we stepped into the area. We began reading the different headstones.

"I didn't realize there were so many."

"Oh, a woman pirate."

"Is this a child?"

We looked. It was for a child about fifteen years old.

"Wow, but it was a different life back then."

"True. My great-grandmother was married at that age."

"Yeah, I've heard this. Sometimes they lied about their age."

We walked through the section a lot more solemnly. It seemed darker somehow. I could almost feel the danger and terror from their life.

"Here it is. The Great Pirate Claude de Palencia."

We stared down at the headstone. It was a bleached white limestone with his name and date of his death carved into it. It didn't list a birth date.

"Hung until dead for crimes of piracy." Amy read. "That's crazy."

"Yeah."

"Different times."

"It's amazing."

I looked around for a clue, but once again, nothing stood out as a clue.

"What the heck do we look for?"

"I knew it wouldn't be easy, but dang, I thought we would see something."

"Wait? What's that?" Denise pointed.

There was a bench with a small sign on it. Donated by the Carren Family Historic Foundation. It had a website under it with a code.

"Is that it?"

"Michael Carren is the guy who started this whole hunt."

I typed it into my phone. It asked for the passcode. I put it in, looking at my friends before hitting enter.

"Congratulations! You have found the last clue. Tomorrow go to the Fort Aston Post Office, tell them you are picking up for William Aston, and then follow the instructions from there."

"Tomorrow!"

"Oh, my gawd!"

"We did it!"

We jumped around, hugging and screaming.

"Wait? Is this the best place to be celebrating?" I asked.

"Ah, maybe not." Amy said.

We giggled, sobered up quickly, and then hurried back to the entrance. We thanked the caretaker as we walked through the building to exit to the parking lot.

Once in the car, we screamed.

"We did it!"

"The first ones to find any of them!"

"I can't believe it!"

"This is amazing!"

"Now what do we do?" I asked.

"We go get plastered drunk and hang by the pool until tomorrow when we go pick up our prize or find out whatever the next clue is." Marissa yelled.

"It's on." We all agreed.

Chapter Twenty-Seven: Marissa

We made a stop at the liquor store.

"Hey, ladies. Y'all look good," Flora greeted us.

"Thanks."

"Are you going to miss us when we leave?" I asked, leaning on the counter.

"When are you leaving?"

"Sunday, so this is probably our last trip here."

"Aw, well, I enjoyed seeing you, ladies." She came around the counter and hugged me. For looking so fragile and frail, she was strong.

"We enjoyed meeting you."

Amy gathered the things she needed to make us another of her mixed drinks. This one was something with rum and ginger beer. She said it was called a dark and stormy. We still had a few limes, which was the only other ingredient needed.

"That'll do it." She said, setting the items on the counter.

"Making dark and stormies?"

"Yeah, I love them."

"You're the one that used to be the bartender, right?" Flora asked.

"That's right. I used to love that job."

"You clearly were good at it." She smiled.

Once the transaction was done, she hugged each of us and then we said goodbye. Back in the car, we made plans for the rest of the day.

"What's the plan for dinner?" Heather asked.

"I say we order delivery."

"I second that."

"Third."

"Alrighty, then, we order something to be delivered." Heather grinned.

We got back to the house, cheered more, and then each went to change into our swimsuits.

I messaged Mike that we'd found the last clue. He was so excited for me. I asked how mom was doing, and he called.

"Hey, babe. I didn't expect you to call."

"Hi, yeah, I thought it was overdue. I should have called you last night."

"What's wrong?"

"Oh, nothing, but they kept her at the hospital. I've been scrambling all day. Between getting the girls to school and their activities, and then coordinating picking up your mom from the hospital today. I have been on the go all day."

"Why did they keep her?"

"They were concerned she might fall again and there were a few spots on the C-scan. They thought she might have broken her hip."

"Oh, my gosh, Mike, what is going on?"

"She's fine. Not a broken hip. Just the wrist, as we told you the other day. She is home now and resting."

"Okay, you sure? Do I need to come home?"

"No, you'll be back in two days. I have everything handled until then, I promise."

"If you're sure."

"Yes, I'm sure." He exhaled. "I really appreciate all you do. This has been an eye-opener to how much you handle."

"I love doing it."

"I know, but I've already talked to the kids, even Emma. You won't be handling everything. I already have Olivia enrolled in driving school. She starts in two weeks."

"Really?"

"Yes. Jackson is going to help with grandpa and grandma more. Olivia is going to work on not depending on you, and Ella, well, she is just going to stay her sweet self."

"And, Emma?"

"She's going to visit more."

I waved a hand in my face to keep the tears at bay, but it didn't work. They were happy tears.

"Thank you."

"Are you crying?"

"No. A little." I laughed through the tears.

"Don't worry. Enjoy the rest of your time off."

"I love you, Mike."

"I love you, too."

We hung up. I sat on the bed, letting the tears fall. It was relief and fear of the change that was coming. My family understood and were going to step up. Emma was going to come home, Jackson was going to help out, Olivia was going to drive, and Ella was going to remain her sweet self.

"Knock, knock." Denise said at my door. "You okay?"

"Yeah, I just got off the phone with Mike. Mom had to stay an extra night in the hospital so they come run more tests, but she's fine."

"So, why the tears?" She sat next to me, putting her arm around me. The simple action made the tears start up again.

"I'm just relieved. They had a family meeting, and everyone is going to step up to help me. All of them, even Emma."

"Really? That's great."

"It is, but you know me. I'm not great with change." I tried to laugh, but it came out as a snort. It caused Denise to laugh, and soon we were both laughing so hard.

"Better?"

"Much."

"Let's go get our drink on." She used a silly voice. She stood and reached for my hand. I giggled as I allowed her to pull me to the party.

Hours later, we had eaten more than our fair share of pizza, had drink after drink of Amy's wonderful creation.

"I can't take credit for this mix either," she said. "I learned it at the bar."

"Well, it is yummy-yummy." I said, as I took another long sip.

"I don't normally drink this much back home." Heather shared.

"No, kidding." Amy teased her.

"I don't either." Denise laughed. "But, with Amy playing bartender, I could get used to this life."

"I could definitely get used to this lifestyle." I said, as I laid back on the lounger.

The late evening sun was just dipping low in the sky, but it was still warm out. Back home in Minnesota, it was still cool. I was going to miss the sunny, warm weather.

"I still can't believe we solved this treasure." Heather squealed.

"I know. It's amazing."

"What do we expect to happen tomorrow?" Heather asked.

"No idea, but we'll find out in the morning." I said.

"I wonder why we couldn't just go straight to the post office today." Amy added.

"And why the post office?" Denise said.

"Do we know where the frat boys are in the hunt?" Amy asked.

"Oh, I almost forgot about them." Heather pulled out her phone. "Unless they didn't share, they are still on the fort clue. That means they still will have to go to the cemetery."

"Well, that's good."

I listened to my friends talk as I just enjoyed my buzz and the sounds of the waves in the distance. After talking to Mike, I was so much more relaxed, even with the worry about my mom. Knowing that my family understood all I did for them and were going to help carry the load without me having to throw a fit about it was a huge load off my mind.

If it worked out, I might not have to give up my job. I loved my job.

I woke up in a chair, darkness all around, except for a low light coming from the kitchen and Amy's phone. She was sitting nearby.

"Oh, good, you're awake." She smiled at me as she set her phone down.

"What time is it?"

"Around 11."

"Oh, I'm so sorry that you had to sit out here with me."

"No, I was happy to. You seemed like you needed the sleep."

"Did I ruin the party?"

"Not at all."

"Thank you." I stood, smiling at her. "I don't know if I've said it yet, but I'm so thankful for this trip and for you all as my friends."

"Aw, sweetie. We love you, too."

We hugged then went inside, parting ways at her bedroom. I was only mildly embarrassed that I'd fallen asleep as I daydreamed. It was sweet of Amy to sit with me. I got ready for bed, then checked my phone. I had text messages from all four of my children congratulating us on finding the treasure. Seeing their sweet messages brought a few happy tears to my eyes.

We hadn't officially found it yet; we'd just gotten through all the clues. Tomorrow was an unknown, but for tonight, I was happy.

Chapter Twenty-Eight: Denise

Usually, the morning after felt like drama and cottonmouth, but I felt lighter and free. It was nice to have my secret out. My friends had taken the news well, which shouldn't have been a surprise. They'd always been so supportive.

Now, I needed to tell Sid and Max. My stomach fluttered at the thought of that conversation. I couldn't decide if I would call her or wait.

Before I could decide, my phone rang. Sidney.

"Hey, what's up?" I answered.

"Good morning, mom. I've got news!"

"You do?"

"I got that job!"

"Oh, Sid, that's awesome. Congratulations."

"Thanks, mom." She giggled. "How's the trip?"

"We found the last clue and we're supposed to go to a post office today for the treasure, I think? We don't know what to expect yet."

"Oh, wow. We both have big things going on."

"Yeah, I guess we do." I paused. "I actually have some other news, not exactly happy news."

"What's that?" The tone in her voice had me second-guessing doing this now, but I took a deep breath.

"I have cancer."

"Oh, mom!"

"I probably should have told you before the trip, but —"

"You knew before the trip? Mom, why didn't you tell me?"

"Yes, I'm sorry. I should have told you, but you know everything we went through with your grandmother, my mother. I couldn't be a burden."

"But you *aren't* grandma. You are amazing and you've done so much for me. I would never say you were a burden."

I knew she was right.

"I know now how silly it was not to say something, but at the time... well, I was just scared, I guess. If I said the words out loud and told people, people I love, that it would really be happening."

"Aw, I love you."

"I love you, too."

"I only have a few minutes before I need to go, but tell me everything."

I spent the next few minutes filling her in on everything, including that I'd have surgery the week after her graduation.

"And Heather will come to take me and stay with me after the surgery."

"That's so sweet of her, but I'll be there, too. Both Max and I will."

"I can't ask all three of you to put your lives on hold for me."

"You aren't. We want to me there. I don't think you realize everything you have done for everyone else."

"Really?"

"Mom, seriously, you supported me my whole life. I can't think of one time that I ever felt let down by you, even those few years in my early teen years when I yelled at you daily."

We laughed. She had a hot temper for a minute there.

"Yeah, made me understand why some animals eat their young."

"That's awful." She laughed. "I need to go, but are you keeping anything else from me?"

"No, that's it. You know all my secrets now."

"Okay, well, no more secrets. You are my best friend and I love you."

"Aw, you're so sweet. I'm so proud of you."

With that, we hung up. It went better than I expected. She had matured into a wonderful young lady.

I stretched, checking the time. Just enough time to hit the bathroom and coffee pot before the sunrise. Today would be our last full day here. Tomorrow we would head home. I couldn't believe this trip was already over and I'd be facing reality.

Despite what awaited me at home, I felt a lot more positive. I guess Dr. Ruiz was right about having a support system. Knowing Heather would be there and now Sidney knows about it, I feel ready to take this on.

"Hey, good morning." I said, joining my friends on the back deck. It was just Amy and Heather so far. "Marissa still sleeping?"

"Yeah." Amy said.

"How long did she end up sleeping out here?"

"Another hour after y'all went to bed, so not too much later."

"Oh, good."

We sat there in peaceful silence, listening to the waves and birds. Out in the distance, there was lightning as a storm seemed to be brewing on the horizon. It was far enough out, that we couldn't hear the thunder that surely followed it, but it made for a beautiful sight.

"Morning, ladies." Marissa said.

"Morning." We all said.

"Sorry that I pooped out on you guys last night."

"No, it's fine."

"We were just hanging out."

"I went to bed not long after you fell asleep."

"Wow, I'm glad I woke up in time for this." She said, pointing to the sky.

"Yeah, it's gorgeous."

"I'm going to miss this the most."

"Yeah, I don't have a view like this back home."

More companionable silence with an occasional glance around at each other. This was friendship. We could be silent and didn't feel the need to speak. We understood each other.

The storm slowly got closer.

"I hope this doesn't put a damper on our last day."

"We need to be at the post office by 9, right?"

"Let's get breakfast at that cute diner down the road."

"Oh, that pink and silver place. I'm in."

We agreed to be ready in forty-five minutes. That should give us plenty of time to get to the diner, eat, and then make it to the post office just in time. As long as the storm stayed at bay.

I was down to the last of my outfits. Today I had on a simple floral sundress. It was flowy and fell right at my knees. I slipped into my sandals. Thankful that we weren't hiking or doing a trek through a cemetery today. Just go to the post office for whatever waited for us there.

I pulled my hair up into a ponytail. With the weather, I didn't want to take the time to fix it up. A little lip gloss and a touch of mascara were all the make-up I ever did. It was just ten years ago that I'd spent fifteen plus minutes doing a full face. I softly laughing remembering all the blending of the foundation, powder, blush, and bright, thick lipsticks. Now it wasn't worth it to me.

I was the first ready, so I took a seat in the living room to wait. Heather soon joined me.

"I'm so excited. I can barely think straight."

"It's exciting."

"I wish I knew what was waiting for us and why they asked us to come at a certain time."

"Maybe they'll have reporters or something to greet us."

"Oh, wouldn't that be something?" She clapped her hands.

"By the way, I talked to Sidney earlier. I told her."

"You did? How did she take the news?"

"She was a little upset that I hadn't told her, but she is supportive."

"You sound surprised."

"No. Well, maybe. I guess I built it up in my head, but if I really thought about it, I would have known she would be."

"We all love you."

"That's what she said. I love you, too."

Marissa and Amy joined us a moment later.

"Ready?" Amy jingled the keys.

We hopped in the car and headed to the pink and silver diner. It was called the Cherry's Diner. Stepping inside, it was like being transported back to a time long gone. The waitstaff was head to toe 1950s diner style clothing in all colors of pinks and turquoise with crisp white aprons.

"Sit anywhere, ladies." One lady with the tallest beehive hairdo I'd ever seen said. "Menus on the tables."

"I love this place." Heather whispered in my ear as we walked through the dining room.

We found a turquoise and black booth near a window. Heather and I sat on one side, with Amy and Marissa on the other.

"This place is cute." Marissa said, passing us each a menu.

"It is. Great job picking restaurants this week." Amy said to Heather.

"It was my pleasure." She grinned.

"Howdy, ladies. What can I get y'all to drink?" A waiter with an Elvis style hairstyle asked.

"Coffee and water, please."

"Just water for me."

"Orange juice and water."

"Only water please."

"Great. Comin' right up."

I watched him walk away, then watched as another bouffant haired beauty sashayed past with a tray loaded with breakfast favorites. The smell of maple syrup and bacon followed behind her.

"I really love this place."

"What's everyone thinking?" Amy asked.

"Short stack with bacon." Heather said.

"I'm leaning towards the two-egg plate with bacon and biscuits." I said.

"That's what I'm thinking too." Amy said. "Breakfast twins."

We laughed.

"So, once again, I'm the last one to decide." Marissa frowned.

Our server came back with our drinks.

"You ladies ready?"

"Everyone else order, I'll decide by the time it's my turn." Marissa said.

We all placed our orders and then stared at Marissa.

"Oh, sorry. I am so decisive in every other area of my life, but food… not so much." She sighed. She looked at Heather. "The short stack with sausage."

"All good choices. It'll be right up."

We sat chatting and enjoying the atmosphere of the 50s style diner. Between the music and the people, it really set a mood.

"I can't believe this is our last day here." Amy frowned.

"I know. It's been so great spending this week with you all."

"It really has. We can't wait this long to do it again."

"Yes, I say we do it each year."

We all agreed.

Our food arrived. It all looked good and smelled better. I was going to savor every last bite of it. It would likely be one of my last treat meals until I was in remission. My entire outlook on my cancer was not as morbid. With my friends and daughter in the know, I had gotten more optimistic about things.

"These are the best biscuits." I said, taking another bite.

"They are." Amy said.

"These pancakes are great, too."

"I can't even think about the food. I'm getting so excited to head to the post office." Heather blurted.

"Me too." Amy laughed. "I mean, I'm enjoying breakfast, but I can't stop thinking about the treasure."

"I wish we knew what to expect."

"Well, we'll never find out if you ladies don't eat," Marissa teased.

"Yes, mom." We all said.

We finished up, settled, then practically sprinted to the car.

"Yay! Treasure time."

"Treasure hunting mamas!"

We made our way through the Saturday morning traffic. Most were heading in the opposite direction as they made their way to the beach.

Ten minutes later, Marissa slid the car into a spot at the post office. From the outside, it just looked like any other US Postal Office. Concrete and brick exterior, flagpole, and two postal boxes for drop-offs.

"Nothing looks unusual or special."

"No media vans or balloons."

"Yeah, I was expecting a little fanfare."

"Maybe we go in so we can see what's what?"

We climbed out of the cooled air of the car into the humid Florida air. It was humid back home, but this was a different level. After a week, I still wasn't used to it.

We opened the door. Nothing special.

"Should we go to the counter?"

"That's what the instructions said."

We got in line. There were only two people in front of us and one at the counter being helped. An older gentleman with one parcel and a young mother with a baby in a stroller. As the line moved and we were next in line, a man came from the back.

"Can I help you, ladies?"

We stepped forward. We looked at Amy to speak for us.

"Yes, we are here picking up for William Aston." Amy spoke for the group.

"William Aston, you say?"

"Yes."

"Are you the Treasure Hunting Mamas?"

"Um, yes?"

"Congratulations!" He yelled.

People came from the back with balloons and confetti. Camera flashes blinding us as a photographer started capturing the moment.

"Oh, wow."

"What?"

"Holy moly."

"This is amazing."

"I'm so excited to finally meet you. I'm Michael Carren." The man who had greeted us at the counter said. He stepped forward with a package. "Here is your prize."

He handed it to Amy. Her wide eyes turned to face us.

"Open it." Marissa said. "You started all this."

"Okay." She giggled nervously.

She tore open the box, revealing the bust of the pirate. She held it up for us all to look at.

"Can I get you four ladies together with Michael?" The photographer asked.

We squeezed together and posed as the photographer directed. A reporter from the local news station started peppering us with questions. Marissa took on the role of answering the questions.

"How did you figure out the clues so quickly?"

"We just put our heads together and looked at each carefully." Marissa said.

"You're some pretty special ladies. How long have you been friends?"

"About twenty years. We met online through a forum for mothers."

"Oh, wow. That's awesome. I joined a group a few years ago. I hope my friendships last this long."

Michael, Amy, and Heather were having an animated conversation that I couldn't quite hear. It seemed he was asking about our journey, too.

"So, what happens with the other team that's here?" I heard Amy ask.

"They will get a certificate of completion. I won't be here to greet them unless they figure it out today. I have a flight out first thing in the morning. There is a team in Washington state on the heels of finding that one."

"That's amazing."

I smiled at Heather. We had beaten the frat boys, and that made us all happy. We were the moms, and we'd done it. The first to figure out his treasure hunt with the first prize. No matter what, no one could take that from us. This was going to be a wonderful memory to think about as I recovered and beat cancer.

Chapter Twenty-Nine: Amy

We stood near my gate as my flight was getting ready to board. I was the first of our group to leave.

"Oh, I'm going to miss you bitches like crazy." I said, hugging each of them.

"Me too."

"Love you, babe."

"See you soon."

We'd already agreed we'd do an annual girl's trip from now on.

"Text when you each arrive."

"You too."

They called my flight to board. I looked over my shoulder towards the gate. While I was excited to get back home, I really didn't want this trip to end. The week had flown by.

I hugged them each once more before joining my fellow passengers in line. Looking back, I saw my friends still standing there watching me. I waved as tears formed in my eyes.

The lady ahead of me in line kept looking back at me. I was about ready to tell her off when she smiled.

"Hey, sorry to keep staring, but didn't you and your friends just find that treasure?"

"Oh, gosh, yes, we did."

"That's amazing. I never thought of doing something like that. You know, you always see young people or old men doing that. Y'all are an inspiration to us all."

"Wow, thank you. It was a fun girls' trip."

I hadn't thought about what we would look like to other people. I mean, I'm sure there were other women our age doing inspirational, adventurous things. Though I had thought about it mostly being young people, like the frat boys that made the news.

Speaking of the frat boys, they gave up when it was reported we found the treasure. They didn't even try to get second place. They simply moved on to the next one on the list. It was a shame really and if that would have been my kids, I would have lectured them for not finishing what they started. They had only been two clues away.

She smiled again as the line started moving. I made my way onto the airplane, to my seat, and after six hours and one plane change, I was arriving back at home. The flight was smooth. Nothing to complain about, except it wasn't Florida with a fruity drink and my girlfriends.

I turned my phone on, and immediately text messages rolled in. One from Marissa. She was already home. She was lucky enough to have a direct flight, so even though she left after me, her travel time was half of mine. Next, I saw Heather was delayed in Atlanta. The last text was from Scott. He was waiting by baggage claim.

My stomach flip-flopped at the thought of seeing him. We'd had good communication the last two days, but I was still nervous. Would we fall back into our old pattern of fighting all the time? His backhanded compliments and my defensive snaps.

I felt more relaxed and ready to work at this. I just hoped he was in the same place.

I shot him off a message that we'd just landed. I grabbed my carry-on and followed the others off the plane. I made a quick stop at the restroom.

As I came down the escalator to the baggage claim, I scanned the crowd. He said he'd be waiting right here.

"Amy." His deep voiced called.

Tears formed in my eyes. It was in that moment that I knew we'd be okay. I ran to him, the best I could in the crowded room.

"Babe." I wrapped my arms around him as he caught me. We kissed.

"I missed you, darlin'."

"I missed you, too."

"Let's go find your bags." He took my hand, and we found the luggage carousal for my flight. "You had two bags?"

"Yes."

My phone chimed. It was Denise getting home.

"Everything okay?"

"Yeah, Denise just got home."

"Oh, good."

The luggage started coming out and people rushed forward, blocking the view.

"Stay here. I'll grab your bags," Scott whispered.

I watched as he moved forward and took a spot near the carousal. He looked back once with a big smile. I waved.

My phone chimed with a reply to Denise from Marissa, so I added a message to the group. Then watched as Scott grabbed my first bag and then a moment later came my second. He turned with a big, triumphant smile.

"Got your bags. Ready to go home?"

"So, ready."

Thirty minutes later, we were pulling into the driveway. I sighed. It was good to be home.

"Archie!" I called as soon as I stepped into the house.

His familiar meow calling back and soon he was at my feet. I picked him up as he began to purr and rub against my chin.

"Hi, buddy. I missed you."

"Aw, he missed you, too."

I smiled at Scott. Normally, he would have said something stupid like, "You love that damn cat more than me." That would have led to a fight, but today, he was sweet.

"I'll put your bags in the bedroom for you."

"You're so sweet. Thank you."

I set the cat down, but he stayed right with me. I followed Scott to our bedroom to find he had spread rose pedals and had a dozen fresh cut ones on my nightstand.

"Surprise!"

"Oh, baby, this is... beautiful. Thank you."

"I really want to get back to a place of happy with us. We are really a good couple."

"We are."

We kissed our way to the bed to reconnect.

The next day, I was feeling happy and relaxed. My marriage would not fail. We were going to make this work.

I hopped in the shower to get ready for work. Scott joined me.

"What are you doing?" I giggled.

"Saving water."

An hour later, I was finishing up my hair about to head back to the office. I had put it all completely out of my mind for the week, not even checking my work emails.

"Ready for reality?" He wrapped his arms around me.

"Ha, not really. I wish I could just stay in my little happy bubble for another week or two or forever."

"Maybe become a treasure hunter full time."

"Wouldn't that be something, but no. It was fun for a week, but I think it was mostly the people I was with."

"Well, good luck. I'll see you after work." He kissed me, then headed to the gym.

I stared at my reflection for a moment. "Why was I not born rich?"

I turned to Archie, who had been by my side since I'd gotten home. He blinked at me.

"I'll be home right after work. I promise." I scratched his chin, then headed out to the car.

I couldn't quite describe how I felt. Maybe rejuvenated. It wasn't until the trip that I really realized how burned out and depressed I was.

Now, I felt lighter and happy. Ready for whatever awaited me at the office and in life.

Chapter Thirty: Heather

After splitting from my friends at the airport, I sat at my gate. On the news, it noted bad weather in Virginia, so my flight out of Atlanta was going to be delayed.

"Darn it." I mumbled.

The trip being over was a little sad, but I had a purpose and wouldn't just be going home to a lonely existence. In two weeks, I'd be going to stay with Denise and help her for the first week after her surgery.

I'd even started researching what to expect with her recovery. Things like what she could eat or what medicines she'd likely be taking. My friends and family would laugh at me, but I liked to have a plan.

I pulled out my phone now and scrolled through the forums for the treasure sight. We were getting glowing accolades from everyone. It was fun to read through them.

I felt a little bad for the young men who had also been looking for this treasure. They gave up and moved on to a different one. If only they knew they would get a second-place win. It wasn't the statue that we received, but it was still, in my opinion, a wonderful accomplishment. If only they'd have finished it, that is.

After an hour of waiting, we finally got boarded and made our way to our layover in Atlanta. This is where we got delayed. I was going to have to wait here for an extra hour.

I messaged Jason and then my friends to let them all know.

Jason replied instantly that he had seen the flight information, so he hadn't made the drive yet to the airport.

I found the restroom first and then found a hot dog restaurant to grab a bite to eat. There was seating nearby, so I took my hot dog and drink to an empty table. I ate and people watched. It killed the time.

After I ate, I walked around doing some window shopping at the various airport stores. I didn't go in or buy anything. It was just fun to move around and look

I was so comfortable waiting around. When I was at home, I had nothing but time on my hands. However, I didn't feel sad this time like I did before the trip. The trip had released all the guilt and self-doubt. I knew I would be okay and figure out this next chapter.

As I made my way to the gate, I watched families traveling. One little tot got away from his mother. I bent down in front of him to stop his escape.

"Hi, little guy. Let's wait for mama." I said to him. He looked at me, then looked back at his mother.

"Oh, thank you so much. He is so fast."

"I completely understand. It takes a village." I smiled, waved, and continued on my way.

I didn't say what I was thinking, which was how fast he will grow, you won't be able to keep up. One day you won't be able to catch him and that it's okay. But I stand by my village comment. He will have teachers, friends, and mentors who will help him grow to his full potential. One day, you'll have to let him go. Even though you'll want to chase after him, you can't. Not this time.

Letting go. That's been my biggest test as a mother, but today I felt like I could do it. I was doing it. My boys were doing all the things that I had raised them to do. I gave them wings, but I hoped they knew I would always be there for them.

Finally, I got to the gate, pulled out my eReader and waited. Hours later, we pulled into the gate in Richmond. I was tired and ready for a shower, but we still had a short drive home.

I sent Jason a message that we'd landed but were still on the plane. He confirmed he was waiting in the cell phone lot.

Jason: Let me know when you get through baggage claim and I'll drive over

Me: Okay. See you soon.

I gathered my things and waited to deplane. Finally, I was through everything and standing on the curb waiting for Jason. I was getting excited to see him. We hadn't talked much while I was away, just a few texts and one late-night call.

His car came into view, but I realized he wasn't alone.

"Oh, my gosh." It was my boys. They were both with their father. Tears welled in my eyes.

Tyler jumped out of the car.

"Hi, mom! I'm so proud of you." He hugged me quickly, then started grabbing my bags.

"Thank you. What are you doing here?"

"I'll explain on the way home. We don't want to hold up the line." He pointed to the other cars.

"Right." I grinned and hopped in the front seat while he got into the back with his brother. "Hi, Cody!"

"Hi, mom. It sounds like you had a great trip."

"I did, and thank you for your help with that clue." I smiled back at my boys. "So, how or why or what... You're both here!"

"Dad thought it would be a nice surprise."

"What about work, school?"

"We can take a few days off for our mother." Tyler said.

"I'm so happy." I sent a message to my friends letting them know I'd landed and added a note that my boys had come to visit.

They replied with happy wishes and to enjoy their visit. My heart could burst. We got home, the boys grabbed my bags and took them to my room.

"We're going to pick up dinner. Back in a few," Tyler said.

I turned to Jason when they left.

"How did you make this happen?" I put my arms around him.

"Tyler called with a question, and I simply asked him to come visit."

I wasn't buying that, but I was going to let them think I believed the story. I went to shower so I would be ready for dinner.

The boys arrived just as I came out, fresh and clean from my trip. They had picked up Chinese from our favorite place.

"I have been thinking about their beef and broccoli for months." Cody said, bringing plates to the table.

I sat at the table, looked around at my family. Jason and the boys were talking about sports. I ate and listened, just soaking in our family time. I rarely joined into those conversations, but I had missed this so much.

This was how life should be, but I also knew that once their visit was over, I'd be okay.

I had my trip to Raleigh to help Denise out to look forward to. I could be there to help my friend. After which, I'd figure out my next chapter after that.

Maybe I'd write a book. It was something I'd thought about doing for a while. I hadn't written much in years, but I used to write a blog.

No matter what I ended up doing next, I knew my friends had my back and would be there to support me. I also knew my boys would be there for me, too. Plus, I had the best husband. I reached over and touched his arm. He looked at me with a bright smile.

"Thank you." I whispered.

"It's the least I could do for the glue that's held our family together all these years."

His comment filled my soul and heart. I looked to Tyler and then Cody. They smiled at me.

"We got the best mom." They both said.

"This is just what my mom's soul needed to hear."

After dinner, we spent the evening playing games as a family and laughing a lot. It was as if the past year or so hadn't happened. I was transported back to those days when they were kids and we'd spend our evenings much like this, at least when they didn't have a game or other activity.

Going to bed that night, I was complete. My heart finally knew that they would always be my little boys, even as young men.

Chapter Thirty-One: Marissa

I had an uneventful flight home, which was good, because I was typically the Queen of Terrible Flights. Canceled flights, delays, airplane issues, and passengers causing issues. I had seen or experienced it all. This trip I'd gotten lucky both ways with no issues. It was a nice change of pace. It gave me hope about the pending changes at home.

After getting my bags, I made the slow trek to my car. I cursed myself a little for not having Mike drive me. If I would have done that, I wouldn't be walking for what felt like miles to my car. Finally, I got to the row with my car. When I reached it, I sighed with relief. Just a thirty-minute drive home and I could see my family.

After my wonderful conversation with Mike about the coming changes, I was eager to see if anything had really changed. Even if it didn't, I felt like I had a plan forward for myself. I was going to say no more, hold the family accountable to handle things themselves, and I was going to take more time for myself.

This trip had me realizing how important self-care was and how much I needed to enjoy the moments, not just get through the day.

With that thought, I turned the radio up and sang along all the way home. It was strange that just this morning; I was in Florida and now I was driving through my hometown in Colorado. Instead of the Gulf of Mexico, I was staring at the Rocky Mountains.

Even though the beach had been fun, I loved the mountains. This felt like home.

As I pulled down our street, my excitement and nerves kicked in. Would I slip back into old habits? Would I go back to enabling everyone? Who knew?

I sat in the driveway staring at our two-story, five-bedroom house with the in-laws' suite attached. I loved this house. We'd moved in when Emma was a baby. I'd brought the remaining three babies home to this house. Then, with luck, my parents would live out their remaining years here.

As I was taking in one last moment alone, my family came running to the car. Ella was the first to reach me with Olivia right on her heals. Olivia was smiling and waving.

That was not the same Olivia I left eight days ago.

I opened the door.

"Mom!" Ella threw herself at me. "I missed you."

"Me too." Olivia said, getting in on the hug.

Before I left, these two would never have touched, even if one of them was on fire. Now they were hugging me together.

"I missed you both, too." I smiled, tears in my eyes.

"Watch out, ladies, I need to kiss my wife." Mike announced.

"Ew."

"Gross."

But they stepped out of the way. I giggled.

"Hi, beautiful." He kissed me. "Bags in the back?"

"Yes." I choked out. His kiss might have been chaste, but it held a promise of things to come.

He nodded to Jackson to help him. They wrangled the bags into the house.

Mom and dad looked on from the doorway, but didn't come to meet me. I grabbed my things and with the girls.

"Hi, mom, dad." I hugged them both.

"Hi, sweetie." Dad said.

Mom simply smiled, then looked up at my dad. That was slightly concerning, but I smiled back and we all went inside.

The house smelled amazingly.

"We made dinner." Olivia grinned over at her sister. "To surprise you."

"Oh, wow. It smells so good."

"Roast chicken, grilled veggies, and scalloped potatoes." Ella said.

"Impressive."

"We already have the table set."

I looked at our table; it was set for eight. Adding up in my head, we were only seven. At that moment, I heard the front door open.

"Hello?" Emma yelled from the foyer.

"Oh, Emma!" I hugged her. "What are you doing here?"

"Dad and I had a nice talk recently, and I realized I should visit more. Maybe work a bit less." She winked at her dad.

He and Jackson had just joined us in the kitchen after dropping my bags in our bedroom. They were discussing some sports team that I wasn't familiar with.

I know Mike had said that Emma agreed to help more, but I didn't realize that included joining us for dinners. I was thrilled.

"I'm so happy to see you." I hugged her again.

We all sat around the table. I looked around at all my favorite faces. This is what life was about. Not working, not running yourself all over town, but this right here. Family. I took it all in and I savored the meal cooked by my two youngest.

"This is excellent, girls." I said to them.

They smiled at each other. I had really underestimated what they could do for so long.

"Marissa, when did you get home?" Mom asked about halfway through dinner.

"Oh, just a few minutes ago. How are you, mom?"

"I'm good. Did you have fun at summer camp?"

She was time-traveling again. It was no use in arguing with her about what year it was. Technically, it was kind of like summer camp, only with adult beverages.

"Yes, it was a wonderful trip. I got to spend time with my best friends and we won the grand prize."

"Well, I'm so glad you enjoyed yourself. I missed you."

"I missed you, too."

After dinner, Emma and Jackson volunteered to clean up, so the rest of us went into the living room. There was a baseball game on. Mom sat next to me, holding my hand and randomly looking at me as if she knew me and didn't know me at the same time.

It was in that moment that I knew I was going to need to step away from work completely. I could possibly do some consulting or maybe stay on the board, but it was time to dedicate myself to caring for her and getting those small moments when she knew me.

Dad looked over once, studying me as if he knew what I was thinking. I flashed him a weak smile. He nodded and turned back to the game.

I'd talk to Mike later tonight, but I knew he would support me fully. With that decision made, I settled in for time with my family and this new chapter of life.

Chapter Thirty-Two: Denise

On the way home from the airport, I made a quick stop at the grocery store. I just needed a few things after being gone for a week. After a week of eating fatty, rich food, I filled my basket with fresh veggies and chicken breasts and fish. I wanted to get back to my new lifestyle of taking better care of myself.

Even if my habits hadn't caused my cancer, I was going to spend the rest of my life doing better. It was the promise I'd made myself.

Pulling into my driveway, I pushed the button for the garage and watched it go up. Home. I sighed. It had been a long travel day with a layover in Atlanta.

I grabbed my groceries, taking those inside, and then coming back out for my bag. I dropped it in the laundry room, so I could start all my clothes. It was what I did: get back to ground zero, so to speak.

After those were going, I put my groceries away. First, I divided my chicken into freezer bags. One piece per bag, so I could take out just what I needed. The fish was already divided, so it just got put away. Next, I washed all the vegetables, cutting up some and putting away others.

With that done, I took my toiletries, shoes, and other things away. It had been a fun trip, but it was good to be home. I thought about my friends going home to their families. They were likely getting to tell them all about their trip. I was alone, without even a pet to talk to.

While I mostly liked my single life, after a week with friends, it made the loneliness harder. Though I'm sure once I got back into my routine, I wouldn't even notice again.

But perhaps I should get a pet. Maybe a cat. Yes, once I got through most of my treatments, I'd get a cat.

With my chores done, I wandered around my house, just ensuring everything was in order. Then settled in front of the television along with my eReader. It would be a night of watching shows while reading.

My phone chimed. It was Sidney.

Sidney: Can I stop by?

Me: Of course.

Sidney: OMW

I read her text, speak as she intended, that she was on her way.

Well, this was an unexpected surprise. I thought.

I read until she knocked.

"Hey, mom!" she said, coming in.

"Hey, baby." I hugged her. "I'm so glad you stopped by."

"Yeah, me too. I missed you."

"Miss you, too." I smiled as we got seated on the couch. "Where's Max?"

"He thought it would be nice for us to visit."

"Aw, he's sweet."

"He is." She smiled. "How was your trip?"

"It was great. We had a lot of laughs and made great memories."

"That's wonderful." She paused. "Why didn't you tell me about the cancer?"

I knew that's why she was here. I owed it to her to talk about it face-to-face.

"I'm so sorry that I didn't tell you sooner. I should have. It wasn't fair to you."

"No, it wasn't. I thought we were a team. That's what you always lectured me about growing up."

"You're right. I just let my childhood trauma get into my head. I was already in shock from the news and then retreated into those memories."

She sighed. "I understand. I don't remember her well."

"She wasn't a very loving mother or grandmother, so there wasn't much to remember."

"Well, I'm sure you will be a wonderful grandmother." She handed me a box.

"What's this?"

"Open it."

I slide the ribbon off, then lift the box's top. Staring down, it took me a few seconds to register.

"Is this...? Are you...? I'm going to be a grandmother?"

"Yes!" She had tears in her eyes. "I just found out yesterday, and I wanted to wait to tell you in person. You know, today."

"Oh, Sid! I'm so excited for you and Max." I hugged her as we both started crying. They were happy tears. We laughed and cried for a minute as she told me about feeling a little off, then realizing she was late.

"Max actually went to get the test for me, then we waited together. It was a sweet moment. One of my favorites."

"Aw, baby, I'm so excited."

"Now, we just need to beat this cancer so you can be the best grandmother."

"Yes. I will. I have too much to live for. You, Max, and this little one." I touched her belly. She giggled. "Can I tell people? Well, my closest friends only."

"Of course! I think of Amy, Heather, and Marissa as more like aunts than friends."

"Great. I'm so excited." I took out my phone, taking a picture of the test and then firing off the picture of my friends.

"I need to get home to Max, but I'm so glad you're back."

"Me too. Take care of you. I'll see you in a few days for your graduation!"

"And then the following week, Heather and I will be right there for your surgery."

"I love you."

"Love you."

She left. I sat there, staring at the back of the door. I was going to be a grandmother.

"Oh, my gosh!" I squealed and danced around the room a little.

My phone started chiming with replies from my friends.

Amy: Congrats! We're both going to be grandmothers this year.

Heather: Oh, wow! Congratulations!

Marissa: Woohoo! Grandma Denise!

Now I just needed to beat the cancer and get a cat, then my life would be complete.

THE END

Before you go: If you loved Decoding Us. You may be interested in my books. By visiting my website and signing up for my newsletter, you will receive a copy of Unsolved Murder, the prequel to my Medium with a Heart, Paranormal cozy mystery series.

www.ejwheltonwrites.com

Made in the USA
Las Vegas, NV
30 December 2023

83715625R00142